BOOK ONE OF THE GUARDIANS

GUARDIANS OF THE DEAD

S.L. WILSON

AMBER
PUBLISHING

Cover design, interior book design,
and eBook design
by Blue Harvest Creative
www.blueharvestcreative.com

GUARDIANS OF THE DEAD

Copyright © 2015 S.L. Wilson

All rights reserved. Except as permitted under the U.S. Copyright Act of 1976, no part of this publication may be reproduced, distributed, or transmitted in any form or by any means, or stored in a database or retrieval system, without prior written permission of the publisher.

This book is a work of fiction. The characters, incidents, and dialogue are drawn from the author's imagination and are not to be construed as real. Any resemblance to actual events or persons, living or dead, is entirely coincidental.

Published by
Amber Publishing

ISBN-13: 978-1508433200
ISBN-10: 1508433208

Visit the author at:
Website: *www.shelleywilsonauthor.com* & *www.bhcauthors.com*
Facebook: *www.facebook.com/FantasyAuthorSLWilson*
Twitter: *www.twitter.com/ShelleyWilson72*

Visit the author's website
by scanning the QR code.

For Lee, Jamie & Ella

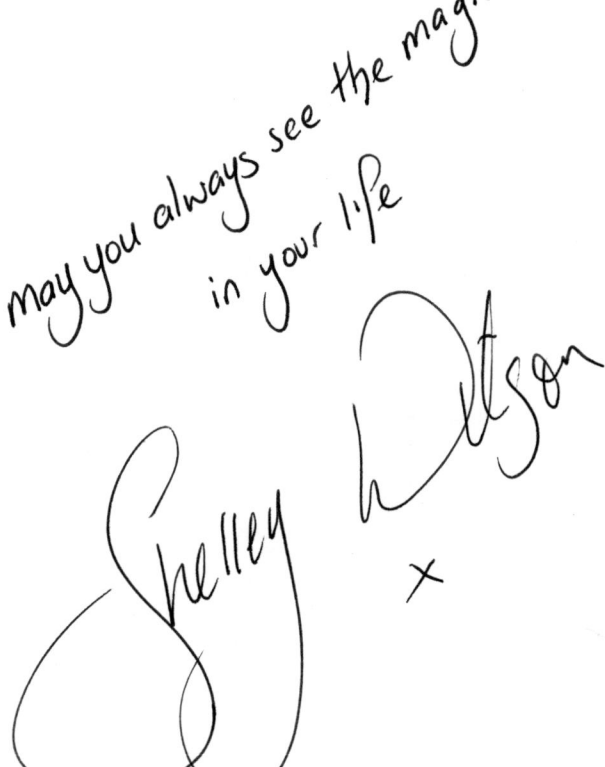

may you always see the magic in your life

Shelley Wilson
x

GUARDIANS OF THE DEAD

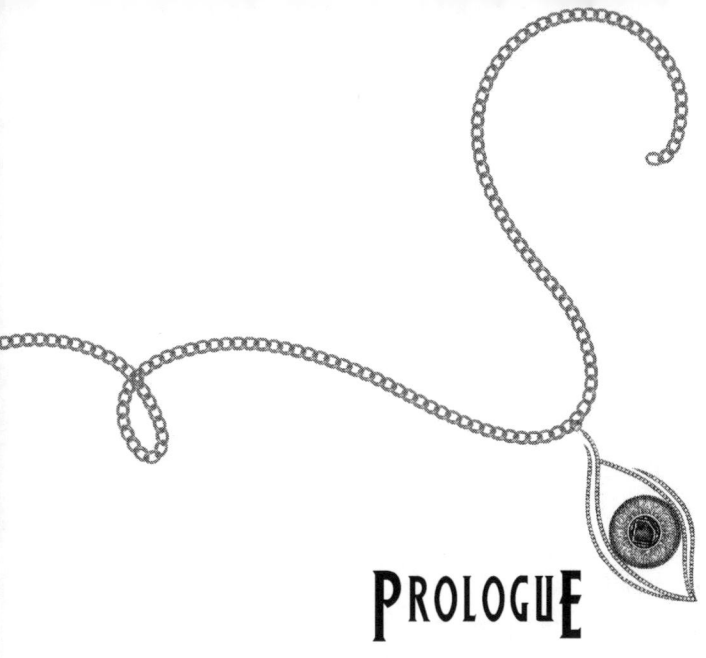

Prologue

Her lungs threatened to burst as she ran, but she pushed herself to keep moving regardless of the pain in her joints. How could she have been so foolish? The signs had been there. The crippling headaches had forewarned her of what was to come but she hadn't heeded the warnings and now she was running for her life.

The old church loomed before her, a humongous sandstone building that, under the light of dawn, appeared to be bleeding from the mortar that sealed the large blocks of stone. The gothic spire soared into the sky, its ornate carvings disfigured by the wind and rain that had hounded it for centuries. If she could make it to the doors she could bind the lock, and cast a spell to prevent anyone getting out.

She had sworn to protect the town which slept around her, its inhabitants safe in their beds. Her own husband and daughter slept soundly, oblivious to her mission.

Her frantic mind calmed as she thought briefly of her daughter. At just six years old she could hold her own against any classroom bully, bright as any scholar and yet she showed no sign of inheriting her family's power. She was a little girl, special in her own unique way but she was no prophecy child. They had been wrong.

Now, as she ran for her life, she feared she may never set eyes on her sweet child again.

The gravel path crunched underfoot as she hurried along to the gaping mouth of the church entrance. Solid oak doors, highly decorated with concentric circles, stood before her, their iron handles caked in rust from centuries of neglect.

The church, once the thriving centre of Hills Heath's community until the disappearances began centuries ago, was now a derelict monstrosity, a haunted mausoleum that the local authority were too afraid to rip down.

She skidded to a halt, dropping to her knees and pulling her heavy coat collar around her neck, protecting herself from the chill of the early morning air. She tried to relax her posture as she cast the protective circle, her heart pounding in her chest as she hurriedly traced the shape in the dirt. Her fingers crackled as blue fire caressed her hands, spreading along each digit until flames danced in her upturned palms.

Pushing her power out, she raised it from the earth, letting it rush through her in a torrent until a lightning bolt escaped and arched towards the wooden doors. Using all her concentration she carved the spell into the wood, splinters of oak breaking off as the blue fire cut deep. Looping the flame in a crescent, she chanted under her breath, drawing her power from the nature surrounding her. She had to prevent them from setting foot in her town. In her world. Time stood still as she heard them approach from behind. The world spun as she realised she was too late and they were already here. The protection spell collapsed as her face smashed into the heavy wooden doors. She tasted blood and wiped her mouth with her sleeve. Shaking her head to try to clear her vision, she stood, sweeping her arms around her, an athame nestled in the palm of her hand.

The dawn mist swirled through the churchyard, cloaking the gravestones. A large shape stepped out from the smog; a tall, muscular man dressed head to foot in black with a golden phoenix emblazoned across his armoured breastplate. His hooded cape was drawn up over his head, disguising all but the hard set of his jaw. From beneath the swathes of black fabric a deep rumbling laugh reverberated across the churchyard.

'I have need of you, witch.' He spat the words at her as he stepped closer, his hand resting on the hilt of the sword hidden from view beneath his cape.

She glared at the huge man. With her dagger raised between them she stood tall with her chin held high. 'My name is Myanna.'

His laugh held no warmth as it echoed in the eerie silence, her blood pounded in her ears, and the tiny hairs on her arms stood erect.

'I don't deal in pleasantries.' He snapped his fingers and two men approached, similarly dressed save for a smaller red phoenix on their armour.

They circled either side of her, cutting off her escape routes. She backed away until her shoulders touched the oak doors. Still clutching her athame and holding it at arm's length she fumbled with her free hand to find the iron handle behind her. There was only one way out. She would have to go through the church.

Planting her feet squarely on the compacted gravel she flung her dagger at the man to the left, striking him in the shoulder as she swung open the wooden door, smashing it into the advancing man on her right. She pivoted on her left foot and slipped through the door, pulling it closed behind her, whispering a sealing spell to slow them down. The inside of the door charred and smoked as the magic took hold.

The interior of the church smelt musty, the years of decay permeating the walls and floors. She was in the nave, an enormous room with vaulted ceilings and rows of wooden pews that faced a raised stone altar. Strings of cobwebs laced across the seats leading to the platform. No-one had stepped foot in there in over two centuries—no-one human anyway. She hurried past the baptistery, once the centre for all the town's christenings, but the font had long since dried up.

SHE SEARCHED along the back wall, running her hands across the stone looking for another exit. An opening in the darkest corner of the church led to a wrought-iron staircase. The stairwell was cloaked in darkness and descended further than her eyes could see. She faltered briefly, unsure if stepping onto the first rung would lead her into more trouble or point her to an escape route.

The heavy front doors of the church smashed open and the men stormed through the entrance with a bloodcurdling cry.

Her time was up. She placed her foot on the first rung and took a step down, then another...

CHAPTER 1

Ten Years Later.

The rasping sound of a match head on stone echoed through the graveyard. The flame spluttered briefly before igniting. As it met with the wick, the black candle burst into life and cast an unearthly green glow across the ground.

The hunched figure scratched whirling patterns on the wet soil with a small chicken bone while pouring hot wax into the grooves. The liquid trickled slowly along the trench until the ancient symbol was alight with green fire.

As the rain began to fall and the sky grumbled, heavy with storm clouds, the figure began to chant.

The symbol shone in the gloom, changing from a ghostly green colour to blood red, blazing like a branding iron against the hide of a dark beast. The thunderclouds rumbled and drowned out the fierce crack of the earth as the ground began to open.

A humourless smile spread across the figure's anaemic face as the soil around the candle trembled. Clots of earth erupted in clumps like macabre molehills and the flames danced in the wind. A sound to the right forced the intruder to squat lower to the ground and nestle between the tombstones to avoid discovery or have the dark magic that seeped into the earth before them halted.

A young couple ran hand in hand through the open church gate from the town square and bolted through the graveyard to the shelter of the trees.

Still laughing from the thrill of her breathless sprint the young girl wrapped her arms around her companion's neck. 'That was fun,' she giggled, giving him a coy smile as she pressed her body in close to his.

The boy's grin spread across his glistening face and he bent forward to kiss her.

As their lips met, the ground around them shook.

'Blimey, Dan, you're a really good kisser.'

He laughed. 'That wasn't me.' He moved away slightly, holding her shoulders as he looked down at their feet. 'It came from underneath us.'

The ground shook again and mounds of dirt spewed forth as if something was pushing up from below.

A flash of lightning momentarily lit up the sky. The earth stirred again, large clots of mud were tossed as high as the gravestones, the topsoil flung to the sky as the earth cracked open and a grotesque creature broke through the surface.

The young girl screamed and stumbled against the tree trunk as her companion stood protectively in front of her. The creature clawed its way from the ground never taking its black eyes off the figures. Long talons with grimy fingernails grabbed at tree roots as it pulled itself from the ground.

The demon was immense. It stood tall and stretched its muscled arms wide revelling in its freedom. It towered over them, its waxy grey skin laced with black veins, its thick neck ending in a horned head with deep set eyes that shone as black as obsidian, jagged teeth filled its mouth and its breath was putrid as it leant down to snarl at the young couple. Dark spots covered its scalp and a row of scars ran from its nose and up across its forehead to meet with the two grey horns.

The girl sobbed. 'What is it?'

Snarling at them, the creature then licked its dirt-covered lips. Skulking forward it swiped a long arm and sent the girl skidding across the ground to crash head first into a headstone. Blood oozed from a deep gash on her forehead and she screamed hysterically, holding her dirty hands to her head.

The boy faced the creature, anger powering his actions. 'Leave her alone!' he screamed.

The creature laughed and, moving faster than the boy could see, leapt through the air to hunch over the hysterical girl like a feral dog over its dinner. In one fluid movement it ripped off her head and tossed it to the ground.

The colour drained from the boy's face as he staggered backwards, a wave of nausea washing over him. He vomited over one of the gravestones then scrambled into a run. He ran blindly, hot tears stinging his eyes. He tripped over tree roots and rocks but never looked back. The overhanging branches of the churchyard's trees clawed at his face as he tore through the night, a heavy weight of grief and panic lodged in his heart.

He could hear the creature gaining on him, its foul odour permeating the night air. Ahead of him was the gravel path which led to the town square and civilisation. His legs were screaming with pain as he pushed himself to go faster.

With the church gate in sight he crashed to the ground in a cloud of wet gravel, the creature's razor sharp talons wrapped around his ankle. He kicked out with his free leg as he was pulled along the path, clutching at tree roots and tufts of grass, writhing to break the bond, but the creature was much stronger.

A lone figure stepped out from the treeline to stand in the demon's path. The man was dressed head to foot in black: black trousers and heavy boots that were strapped up to his knees with leather cord, and a long cape covered an armoured breastplate with a picture of a red bird at the centre. The hood of the cape was drawn up over the man's head obscuring his identity. In his hands he held two curved swords which he lifted slowly and pointed at the demon.

The creature snarled and easily tossed the boy to the side as it faced its new opponent.

With a bloodthirsty roar the monster threw itself at the man, its talons slashing wildly as it tried to slice him in half, but he was too fast. He sideswiped the creature and hacked down with his right sword catching its left flank. Green ooze poured from the open wound and the creature howled into the night. The man circled in front and thrust his sword up into the creature's belly, simultaneously slicing its throat with his other weapon.

The huge lumbering creature fell silent and crashed to the ground. Its skin began to burn and sizzle and within minutes the immense fiend had been reduced to ash, washed away by the heavy downpour which continued to pound the earth.

The boy watched as the mysterious hooded figure surveyed his surroundings while he cleaned his blades on the hem of his cape, his face still hidden under his black hood.

He tried to stand but his shaking limbs wouldn't work, instead he dragged himself over to the churchyard wall and leant against the cold, wet stones, fighting to stabilise his breathing as he wiped the fresh blood from the cuts on his hands down his trouser leg.

The man slotted his swords back into their sheaths and strode over to where the boy was sitting, half on the ground and half propped against the wall.

'Thank you,' Dan said, his voice muffled as he wiped the vomit from his mouth with the back of his hand.

The figure swivelled his head to look out once again across the graveyard. Someone was there but before he could react or call for help the man crouched down beside him, bringing his face within inches of his own. He pulled out a pencil-thin dagger, the blade not much wider than a needle. The handle was made of a translucent material filled with a murky purple liquid.

Without warning the man dropped his hood. His shaved head was covered with an ornate tattoo which wound over his scalp and trailed down his neck. His features were chiselled and hard. Deep, ruby red eyes looked back at Dan, glowing in the darkness like pools of fire.

He took hold of the blade in his right hand and placed it over the boy's chest.

'No, wait!'

The man studied Dan for a long moment then plunged the blade into the boy's heart. As it reached the hilt, the murky substance that had filled the handle drained into his body and the hot liquid seeped into his bloodstream.

Before Dan blacked out he saw the great oak doors of the old church loom up ahead of him. The church that had been derelict for years. As he drifted into unconsciousness he wondered if he would ever see those oak doors again.

AMBER NOBLE tucked her brown curly hair behind her ears and folded her coat tightly across her chest, protecting her from the night air. It was threatening to rain as she hurried along the deserted street, eager to get home and out of the cold.

She checked her watch, ten thirty; she was in so much trouble.

'Get a job,' her dad had told her, *'I'm not having you sitting around all summer getting under Patricia's feet.'*

As if she would want to get under Patricia's feet. Her loathsome stepmother had lined her up with a desk job at the local beauty spa; Amber shuddered at the thought: an entire summer wasted with that woman and her plastic, peroxide friends. She sourced her own job as soon as possible but even that had caused a massive argument. Her dad hadn't spoken to her for two days, much to Patricia's delight.

Working at the local coffee shop apparently wasn't good enough for Alan Noble's daughter, but then these days nothing she did was ever going to be good enough for her father.

The sleepy eyes of the shop windows ended and Amber cut across the town square in the direction of the old abandoned church. Its dark, grey bulk was an ugly blemish on a quaint English town.

As she hurried past, she glanced at the stone archway framing the oak doors, which yawned like a mouth from the house of horrors at the funfair. The similarity had always unnerved Amber and the recurring nightmares of her mother being sucked through those church doors into a flaming inferno still haunted her ten years after her mother had walked out on them.

The sky rumbled as it began to rain. Pulling her coat tighter, Amber skirted around the grey walls.

The spire of the old building glistened in the downpour and was briefly illuminated in a flash of lightning. It gleamed a dull red in the night sky, like the bloody end of a sword.

The walls towered above her as she splashed through the puddles. At the crossroads of Orchard Street and Station Avenue, she turned right heading out of town. The graveyard walls fell away to waist height and Amber could see across the black headstones to the rear of the church.

As another flash lit up the sky Amber saw a figure run behind the stones, a fleeting vision of black and silver. She slowed her pace.

Squinting into the gloom she watched for signs of movement. A flash of silver caught her eye and she concentrated hard on the space between the headless angel and the oak tree that dominated the cemetery.

There was someone out there, dressed in black with a hoodie pulled over their face.

Crackheads. As she pushed away from the wall, a sudden scream filled the air. She grabbed for the stone and scanned the cemetery for the hoodie addict to emerge again, worried he had lured an unwilling victim to his crack den.

A low howl filled the air as if a dog were being neutered. The hoodie passed across her line of sight again and Amber saw that what she had assumed was a wayward teen was a heavily muscled man. The heavy 'hoodie' was in fact a long black cape covering black trousers, heavy boots and an armoured breastplate with a picture of a red bird at the centre.

As if the man sensed an audience he swivelled his gaze at her. Blood red eyes peered out from the gaping hole beneath his hood and she felt his fierce stare drilling into her. She gasped as the figure lifted up two curved blades. Bile rose up in her throat as she spied thick liquid ooze down the silver. The man whirled the swords in his hands and wiped the mess on the hem of his cape.

Amber's legs were shaking as she backed away from the church wall. The hooded man continued to watch her, his red eyes following her like a kestrel watches its next kill.

She lurched backwards, covering her mouth with a trembling hand, as the mysterious stranger hunched down over something lying at his feet. She set off running, tripping over her own shoes in the rush to get away. She didn't dare look back, only concentrating on getting home in one piece.

PATRICIA TWITCHED the curtains briefly as she paced the living room. Ten o'clock the girl was supposed to be home and still no sign. The street was in darkness and the excessive rainfall caused tiny rivers to flow along the kerb and bubble up in the grates. The thunder rumbled as Patricia finally spotted a drenched figure running down the street.

She pursed her lips and crept out into the hallway. The door to the office stood open and Alan Noble was busy at the computer as she draped her arms around his neck and planted a kiss on his cheek.

'You work too hard,' she purred. 'If only that daughter of yours appreciated what you do and had the decency to be home when she promised. My poor lamb, you must be so worried.'

Alan glanced at his wristwatch, 'It's nearly eleven, Pat. Isn't she home yet?'

'Not yet, sweetie, but I'm sure she'll have a wonderful excuse *this* time.'

The front door crashed open and Amber burst into the hallway, dripping wet from head to toe. Her long dark curls hung limply around her face.

'Dad!'

'Have you seen the time, young lady?' he boomed, cutting her off mid-sentence and standing up from his desk. 'This is the third time you've been late this week, Amber. That coffee shop woman is taking advantage.'

Amber tried again to speak, but her dad was clearly on one of his rants. There was no hope of getting a word in when he was like this.

She looked past her father's shoulder and spotted Patricia perched on the side of the desk. Her perfectly groomed hair was scooped into a flamboyant updo; she wore a pink Juicy Couture tracksuit with matching manicure and pedicure and was smirking.

Bitch. Amber realised she had been played; her dad would only break off from his work to notice her absence if he was interrupted.

'...and if you think you are going to keep working at that coffee shop then you're mistaken.' Her dad carried on with his ranting but Amber snapped to attention as he finished his sentence.

'I love that job, Dad, I'm not going to quit.'

She crossed her arms in a defiant gesture, the same pose she had used since she was six years old and he had told her she was getting a new mummy.

'It's late, sweetie pie, why don't we all sleep on it?' Patricia wound her arms around her dad's waist and rested her head on his shoulder, 'I'm sure Amber will see sense in the morning.'

The cold stare she gave Amber made her shiver more than her rain-soaked clothing.

Amber headed for the stairs. 'I'm going for a shower.' She ran up them two at a time before her dad could start another argument.

SLAMMING HER bedroom door she slumped back against it, the memory of what she had just witnessed at the graveyard still sharp in her mind.

Her heart hammered in her chest as she visualised the man with the red eyes, the screaming and howling. The events were horrific enough but what worried Amber more was the fact that she had seen this scene before. The dreams that invaded her mind every night were getting intense. They weren't a muddle of images anymore, they were short visions that she couldn't escape from. Only when the nightmare came to its gruesome end could she wake up, but this was the first time she had seen her vision happen in reality.

She felt sickened and yet she realised that, strange though it seemed, the run-in with her dad had upset her more than the horror she had just witnessed at the churchyard.

They were arguing more and more lately. She couldn't do anything right. Patricia was always at her dad's side exploiting the ill feelings between them. They had been so close before her mum left; a happy family who did happy family things like picnics and day trips. Then one day everything changed and she was gone. No note, no sign – she just vanished early one morning.

The police were sympathetic and searched for a few weeks, but with no leads there was nothing they could do but abandon the case. She'd left everything behind: clothes, shoes, make-up and all the sentimental stuff like family photos, trinkets and jewellery. It was as if she'd wanted to cut Amber and Alan out of her life. Her dad met Patricia soon after and moved her in straightaway with no discussion or family conference. She had gone through the house like a tornado, throwing out anything that had belonged to her mum.

AMBER WRIGGLED out of her wet jeans and T-shirt and padded down the hall to the bathroom. It felt good to stand under the hot stream of water. She scrubbed her skin as hard as she could manage, trying to wipe away the memory of what she'd witnessed, but every time she closed her eyes the image of the red-eyed man appeared.

She was exhausted when she finally collapsed into bed. This was her sanctuary; Patricia had re-vamped the entire house so it now resembled one of those minimalistic show homes from glossy magazines. The carpets, walls and furniture were all white, and Amber was petrified to sit anywhere in her own home.

Her bedroom, however, remained untouched; after yet another blazing row, her dad had agreed that Amber was old enough to decorate her own room. She hadn't changed a thing. She kept the tatty pastel wallpaper with the tiny pink rosebuds, the pink curtains and even the threadbare pink rug on the floor. Her mum chose those things and she wasn't ready to get rid of anything from a happier once upon a time. Her stuffed animals crowded together on top of her free-standing wardrobe, keeping a silent vigil, and her exam schedule from last term was still taped to the door.

To the right of her bed was a small alcove with a built-in desk her dad made when she was five. The shelves which filled the wall space were full of books and picture frames – the only photographs of her mother in the house.

As Amber lay in bed she could see the moon through her window. Her eyes were beginning to droop when a movement outside the glass made her heart freeze. She slowly leant over and turned off the lamp, plunging the small room into darkness. She waited for her eyes to adjust to the gloom and carefully edged over to the window, peeking around the curtain to see outside.

A shadow loomed up against the glass and Amber jumped, clasping her hand to her mouth to stop from screaming and waking her dad. Her heart hammered in her chest as the shadowy figure knocked sharply on the windowpane.

Since when do mysterious red-eyed men knock?

Tearing back the curtains she unlocked the window and swung it wide open.

'About time, it's freezing out there. English summers aren't what they used to be.'

Tom threw his leg over the ledge and hopped through into Amber's room. His blond hair was plastered to his head by the rain instead of in its usual perfectly coiffed spiky ensemble. He kicked off his trainers, discarded his coat and curled up on the bed like a cat waiting to be tickled.

'Hey, cutie,' he smiled up at Amber, 'thought I'd pop round for the gossip, heard you shouting halfway down the street and figured you may need a shoulder to cry on.'

Amber laughed and snuggled up beside him on her bed. She and Tom had been best friends forever, their mums were in the same maternity ward, they went to the same schools and they had lived next door to each other all their lives. They were inseparable – something else Patricia disapproved of and consequently, so did her dad.

'What happened this time?'

'I was late…again.'

'Plastic Patsy wouldn't have liked that then.' He mimicked Patricia filing her nails with a sour expression and Amber laughed.

'She didn't. The bitch must have spurred Dad on again and as usual he went off like Mount Vesuvius.'

'So how come you were late? Up to no good?' He winked and Amber felt her cheeks flush even though she was totally innocent of any debauchery.

'I wish… That would have been less traumatic than what happened to me tonight.'

She filled him in on the strange red-eyed man and the sounds from the cemetery, her fears that she may have witnessed a murder and that no-one would believe her story of visions merging with reality. All the talk of strangely dressed soldier men with swishing swords sounded like a bedtime horror story.

'It's weird talking about it now, it doesn't feel real.'

'It sounds pretty damn real to me.' Tom shivered involuntarily and grabbing the throw from the end of the bed, he covered both of them and cuddled Amber close.

'Don't worry, cutie, we can check it out tomorrow in the daylight and if there's anything strange up there we'll report it. Probably best to mention it to your boss too so she doesn't keep you late again.'

'Thanks, Tom.' She rested her head against his chest, her eyes growing heavy as Tom held her in his arms. He was like a big brother, guardian angel and surrogate mother all rolled into one, and as she drifted off to sleep she couldn't imagine life without him.

THE OLD *oak doors of the church creaked open, and she could make out the fiery pit beyond. Clinging to the ancient headstones she fought against the force that was trying to pull her in. She saw her mother walk in the direction of the doors. She smiled at Amber but her smile faded and then she was screaming. A hooded figure appeared at the doors and pulled her through, tossing her body into the flames. The scene shifted and all Amber could see was a line of young men, all a similar age to her. The hooded man pulled them inside the doors as they cried out in terror. There were hundreds of them, boys lined up one after the other, chained by their feet and hands. Some wore jeans and T-shirts while others wore outfits straight out of her history books. The hooded figure tossed them*

into the fiery pit with ease. As he shifted, his hood fell back to reveal a tattooed scalp. He snapped open his eyes and stared straight at Amber. She screamed.

CHAPTER 2

The previous night's heavy downpour had been replaced with bright sunshine, and the air smelt fresh and earthy as Amber and Tom retraced her steps down the road to town. Her shift didn't start until ten but with her dad still giving her disapproving looks and Patricia bending and stretching with her yoga instructor, Amber had made a quick getaway, grabbing Tom on the way.

Amber regaled Tom with her unusual dream as they made their way along Station Avenue, the tall poplar trees stretching upward like roadside centurions marking their path. They planned to grab a coffee and a breakfast roll before Amber started work, and Tom hinted at the need for an in-depth discussion about possible brain diseases she may have developed. Amber laughed and dug him in the ribs, but they were silenced by the scene that unfolded as they approached the cemetery. The church grounds were teeming with police, a row of white tents had been set up along the gravel path and the whole area had been cordoned off with police tape. Men in masks and white jumpsuits were walking at a snail's pace through the gravestones, their eyes fixed on the ground below them.

'Move along, please,' an officer ordered them.

Tom nodded his head in the direction of the church. 'What's going on?' Even though they both had their suspicions, he couldn't help but ask.

'Nothing to worry about, just a disturbance, move along.'

Amber laced her fingers through Tom's and he squeezed tightly to reassure her. There was quite a crowd gathered by the front of the church; every town resident appeared to have turned up to find out what had occurred under their noses. Tom positioned himself right at the front, as close to the action as possible, and started chatting to a couple of girls from their school. Amber watched the group of men in white jumpsuits as they huddled close to the spot where she had seen the mysterious hooded man the previous night.

'This is *evil* of an epic nature.' He pulled on her arm and looked around him wildly as he steered her away from the crowds. 'They've found Kelly Timpson's body in the cemetery...'

Amber was stunned for a moment; she didn't know what she had expected but it certainly wasn't the body of a girl who shared her maths textbook on a daily basis.

'That can't be right,' she started to say, but Tom cut her off with a flourish of his hands to add, '...without her head!'

Amber felt that all too familiar wave of nausea rise again; she crumpled to the pavement without a care for any passer-by and stuck her head between her knees. Tom crouched next to her and rubbed her back affectionately.

'Sorry, cutie, there really wasn't a delicate way to break that kind of news.' He raised his eyebrows and smiled as Amber struggled with the urge to vomit all over the town square.

'Just a shock,' she murmured, wrapping her arms around herself.

The other girls made their way over to where Tom and Amber were sitting; they looked gaunt, and Amber recognised them as Kelly's best friends. She nodded her head at them in a sign of greeting and sympathy. To her surprise they settled down on the floor next to them.

'So Tom's filled you in then?' Cassie, the thin blonde one spoke first. 'It's so awful, Kelly was so excited about the summer holidays. She and Danny were heading off to travel but now he's missing and she's…she's…' The sobbing started again and Cassie collapsed into her friend's arms.

A cold trickle of fear rolled down Amber's spine. Kelly was dead and her sixteen-year-old boyfriend was missing. Her vision of the line of teenage boys being tossed into the flames resurfaced briefly.

'The whole town's on lockdown,' Tom told them. 'All the shops are closing and the police are telling everyone to stay in their homes until they catch who did this.'

'Maybe we should do as they say then.' Amber stood and dusted down her jeans. Her hands were shaking and the pressure that had built up in her head was threatening to knock her off balance.

'We need to get out of here.' She grabbed Tom's wrist. 'Now!'

They exchanged condolences with Kelly's friends once again and moved off down the high street. The hairs on the back of Amber's neck prickled and she felt the eerie sensation of being watched. She glanced over at the cemetery, half expecting to see the creepy red-eyed guy waving at her from behind the tombstones; instead she spotted Patricia through the crowds.

As their eyes met, Patricia gave a little wave. Amber jerked her head in acknowledgment, 'We have to move,' she said, keeping her voice low and pulling Tom along after her.

THE HIGH street was full of people standing in small huddles gossiping about the 'accident' at the cemetery. Many of the shops had already closed, more out of the morbid curiosity of their owners than as a mark of respect. Even the coffee shop was deserted.

'Guess I have a day off,' Amber muttered under her breath as they stood outside the empty shop.

'There is one place we could go, somewhere we may find an answer to why you dreamt about the church the night Kelly died.' Tom's expression was sheepish as he inclined his head and nodded to the small alleyway adjacent to the coffee shop.

'You're kidding, right?'

He gave her a sly smile and grabbed her hand. 'It's a magic shop, cutie, and they may just know something about your red-eyed friend.'

He pulled her down the short alley until they stood in front of a well-worn wooden door. It looked very much like the type of building you drew as a child, with a green front door in the centre and two picture windows on either side. The windows were cluttered with merchandise; candles of all shapes, sizes and colours were stacked to the left surrounded by books on mythology, folklore and magic spells. The right-hand window display was a little more mainstream with hand lotions, soaps and practical gifts.

A tiny bell chimed as Tom opened the door and they stepped inside.

'Welcome,' a musical voice wafted down from the mezzanine floor. Amber glanced up and saw the store's owner leaning over the railing.

India Saks was probably one of the most enchanting women Amber had ever seen. She always wore elaborate gowns, evidently indulging an air for the dramatic dress-up witch look. Although Amber had seen her around town they had never spoken. She and Tom had a silent understanding that he wouldn't tell her about his interest in Wicca so that she couldn't offend him by calling it hocus pocus.

When India floated down the tiny wooden staircase she looked like a royal princess arriving at a dance, her jet black hair hanging loose and tumbling around her shoulders. She wore a fitted purple dress which swished along the floor as she walked; it laced up down the front like a corset, with a low-cut neckline to show off her creamy skin. Her arms were covered in long black fingerless gloves; she tinkled as she walked due to the number of silver bangles on her wrists. A black choker necklace with a huge blue stone in the centre completed the look.

'Good morning, Tom, nice to see you as always.'

Tom smiled and gave Amber a gentle shove in the back. She scowled at him before summoning all her strength to introduce herself without laughing.

'Hello, Miss Saks, I'm Amber Noble. Tom has told me so much about you.'

India smiled and rested a delicate hand on Amber's shoulder, motioning for them to sit on the green sofa which nestled under the staircase, surrounded by huge volumes of the books she sold.

'A non-believer seeking help, today *has* been full of surprises. You're okay, my dear, I won't bite…or turn you into a frog.'

Tom laughed out loud as Amber's skin flushed, but India's gentle smile showed her she wasn't about to be judged. A lesson that Amber accepted graciously.

'After I finished work last night, I saw something…something weird in the old cemetery.' Amber gave a dry cough then carried on. 'I saw a hooded man with curved swords and red eyes. When we walked past this morning the whole area was crawling with police.'

'What do you know of the history of Hills Heath?'

Amber was confused by the change of direction India's question had taken. 'Only what we were taught in school. The town was founded in 1277 by a priest and grew over the decades due to its close proximity to the river and rail…'

India cut her off mid-sentence. 'Not the school's version, I mean the *true* version.'

She stood and sauntered over to the bookshelves at the rear of the shop. They covered the entire back wall, apart from one doorway which Amber assumed led to a storeroom. She scoured the top shelf and pulled out a thick, leather-bound book before joining Amber on the sofa. The front of the book had a picture of a red bird at the centre and Amber pressed her hand to her mouth as she recognised the image.

'That bird…I saw it last night on the red-eyed man's armour.'

India nodded and ran her fingers across the cover. 'It's a phoenix. They represent renewal and resurrection.'

'It didn't look like this guy was resurrecting anyone, I think he murdered someone, I heard a scream and I saw something on the ground. It was so dark and it was raining, but I know what I saw and seeing the police this morning…well, the news is a classmate of ours has been killed.'

India's face was expressionless as she listened. 'How old was the boy who died?'

'It wasn't a boy, her name was Kelly.'

India shook her head. 'You must be mistaken.'

'There's no mistake, it was a girl who died, but her boyfriend is missing.'

India opened the book and flicked through a few pages until she found what she was looking for, then she held the page out for Amber. 'Is this hooded figure what you saw?'

A colour picture dominated the page; a tall man dressed head to foot in black armour, a long cape flowing down his back and a hood drawn up over his head. His face was stern and twisted into a grotesque snarl and his eyes were red balls of fire. You couldn't make out his feet as he was standing amongst bright orange and red flames which weren't burning him but instead looked to be a part of him. His curved swords were on show under the cape and he held a strange black shield with tiny green flames dancing along its surface.

'Yes, that's the guy but he wasn't so…flame boy, last night.'

Tom peered over her shoulder at the picture. 'Who is he?'

'They are called the Guardians of the Dead, an army of soldiers who keep the demons below ground in their cells.'

'Whoa!' Amber held up her hand. 'Demons?'

India smiled and relaxed back against the sofa, 'Tom was right to bring you here today. I know you mock what I do, Amber, but there are forces surrounding us that a normal human couldn't ever comprehend.'

Amber blushed and looked at her feet. 'I didn't mean to offend, I just don't believe in other forces…or demons for that matter.'

'How do you explain what you saw last night then?'

She crossed her arms across her chest. 'Red contact lenses and a fancy dress outfit!'

'Perfect, so if you're right, then why are you here?'

Amber looked from India to Tom and back again. It hadn't been her idea to come to the magic shop in the first place, but Tom believed that this woman could help and so she needed to be honest.

'I'm here because I think I saw what happened last night…before it happened. I have dreams that are so realistic they frighten me, but they've never come true, until now.'

India smiled and traced a perfectly manicured fingernail along the picture of the phoenix. 'Magic does exist, Amber, and if this can be true then the possibility of other creatures such as demons, also exists.'

Amber scanned the small store; glass cabinets ran along the far wall, full to overflowing with jars and glass bottles of every shape and colour imaginable. In front of the window was a mahogany table displaying huge chunks of crystals, shells and charms. Another cabinet beside the staircase housed hundreds of crystal tumble stones in every possible colour. From the railings of the mezzanine floor hung dreamcatchers in all sizes, some made with feathers and others with crystals. Hand carved wands and spell books were displayed in the glass counter below the old-fashioned till.

'No offence, Miss Saks, but love spells and protection trinkets are just for the weak-minded, it's all hocus pocus.'

India rolled her eyes and with a quick snap of her wrist she sent the book she had been holding floating up to the ceiling. A quick turn of her fingers and the book returned to its spot on the shelf.

Amber swore and jumped up, stepping away from India. Her eyes flashed between the woman and the bookshelf as her mind whirled trying to comprehend what she had just seen.

The door at the back of the store flew open and a dark-haired boy stepped through, his thick brown hair falling across his eyes as he struggled with the box he was carrying. The muscles on his arms flexed as he jostled his way through the doorway.

Amber hopped back another step.

'Hey, Tom.' He looked across at Amber and smiled. 'You brought a friend, what fetches you guys to my domain?'

Amber's head was reeling: floating books, Guardians of the Dead and demons. She didn't know if she had the strength to act naturally in front of anyone else right now, especially someone so gorgeous. Her inability to string a sentence together in the presence of boys (Tom excluded) had always hindered her when it came to getting a boyfriend.

Tom quickly introduced them. 'Connor, this is Amber. Amber, this is Connor, India's nephew.' They shook hands and Connor's warm smile put her at ease.

She studied him as India and Tom filled him in on Amber's sighting last night and on the police activity at the cemetery. His navy T-shirt hugged his torso and pulled tight across his stomach where he had hooked his thumbs into the pockets of his jeans. He didn't look much older than she was but he didn't go to their school. She would have remembered seeing him around the halls. His hair curled up slightly at the nape of his neck and she made every effort to stop herself from reaching out to see if it was as soft as it looked.

'Guardians.' His gravelly voice pulled her out of her daydreams as he made a statement rather than pose a question.

'I'm afraid so,' India answered, as she searched the bookshelves again and pulled out a couple of thick volumes.

Everything was moving in slow motion for Amber as she watched the three of them move around the store.

He didn't even flinch when he found out about the red-eyed guy, she thought.

India began to pile book after book on the tiny coffee table: mythology, demonology, spells and potions. Thirty seconds ago Amber had been a fairly normal sixteen-year-old with a neurotic dad and a malevolent stepmother, now she was struggling to hold herself together in the aftermath of being told everything she believed was untrue, magic did exist and she was in the presence of a bona fide witch.

The sound of India's musical voice tore her from her thoughts.

'You must promise me, boys, stay away from the church.'

Tom and Connor nodded in unison then returned their attention to the growing mountain of books on the coffee table.

Amber shook her head. *Stay away from the church?*

'Why?' She looked at the boys' trusting faces and directed her question to India. 'Why do they have to stay away from the church?'

India levelled her eyes at Amber.

'You may need to sit down for this…' She gestured for Amber to join her on the sofa. 'The Guardians live in another realm to our own, in a land called Phelan. They stole these lands from demons, brutally massacring thousands of them. The demons tried to flee Phelan and during the thirteenth century they began to enter our human realm. An ancient order of witches made a pact many hundreds of years ago with the Guardian general that his soldiers could use our land to imprison the demons and guard against them escaping or roaming free. The demons they didn't kill were imprisoned and the prisons lie directly beneath your feet – in the earth.'

Amber instinctively looked down and shifted her feet from side to side as if the floor had suddenly heated up.

'Don't worry,' Connor chuckled. 'They're in the cemetery ground, not here.'

India went on. 'The gateway to Phelan lies deep within the earth, along with the prison cells. It's the Guardians' job to make sure the demons don't get out and to kill the ones who try to escape. The Guardians are deadly fighters so none of these creatures have ever escaped during my lifetime.' She flipped open one of the books she had in her hands and showed Amber a set of drawings.

The picture showed the town's old church surrounded by human-looking gravestones, but as her eyes travelled down the page she saw that beneath the foundations lay a stone prison, a deep cylindrical vault cut into the rock. A spiral staircase ran through the centre, directly under the church, and descended deep into the earth's core until it ended at a wall of flames.

India pointed at the flaming gateway. 'This is the door to Phelan. Only Guardians can pass through the wall of fire as their general holds the only gateway key.'

Amber's head began to swim; all this talk of demons and Guardians on an empty stomach wasn't good.

India seemed not to notice her distress, or chose to ignore it, and continued, 'The pact has held for centuries, the Guardians keep the demons under control and this town remains oblivious to what goes on beneath its feet. However, there is a catch. The general of the Guardians requested a payment for keeping our realm demon-free.'

'Payment?'

'Yes…to recruit members for their army they require a sacrifice.'

Amber felt drained as the words began to sink in. 'Recruit members for their army,' she repeated very slowly, not really wanting to hear the rest of India's history lesson.

'I'm afraid so. The Guardian general was forged in the heart of a volcano by very dark magic thousands of years ago. He built his stronghold at the top of the Black Mountains and amassed his army from scratch using his blood magic and host bodies.'

Amber began to feel agitated.

'The Guardians take human hosts from our realm, and using this blood magic they undergo a transition to become Guardians themselves, losing any human memories and becoming demon fighting machines.'

Her limbs became heavy and numb, and a wave of nausea and dizziness washed over her. *Yes, that's one history lesson I could have lived without,* she thought as the blackness enveloped her.

WHEN SHE opened her eyes she found herself cradled in Connor's arms. His face hovered over hers, and his handsome features were scrunched up as he frowned in concern. His dark brown hair tumbled into his eyes, and Amber had to fight the impulse to smooth it back with her hand.

'She's awake,' he shouted out, looking behind her towards the door.

India appeared, carrying a wet towel and a mug of something steaming. She knelt down beside her, and Connor gently lifted her up. Holding the hot liquid to her lips she instructed her to take a sip.

'Ugh.' Amber wrinkled her nose and pulled away. 'That's gross.'

Connor laughed and released his grip on her, much to her disappointment.

'She'll live.' He sat back on the floor, wrapping his muscled arms around his knees.

'By the goddess, Amber, you gave me such a fright.' India looked flushed; her milky skin was tinged red and beads of sweat shone on her forehead.

'I'm sorry, I guess all that talk of demons finished me off.'

Despite the sour taste, Amber took another sip of the hot liquid, her mind still swimming.

She cleared her throat, 'I get that the Guardians recruit people to boost their ranks, and then they all fight the demons, but what I don't understand is what it has to do with Tom and Connor staying away from the church.'

'Hills Heath's derelict old church holds the gateway to Phelan, it's the picture from the book. The payment made from the town to the Guardians has stood for hundreds of years. It's a pact and a bargain made with the town's founder, Father Ashby, and upheld by generations of witches' covens. Only one witch refused the payment and she vanished and was never seen again. The Guardians stop demons entering the human realm in exchange for three human sacrifices – sixteen-year-old boys.'

Amber was stunned and snapped her head round to look at Connor. He shrugged his shoulders and gave her a crooked smile. His arm muscles were tense under his sleeves. As he sat hugging his knees to his chest, his brown eyes watched her reaction, and she thought she saw admiration there.

'It's a lot to take in,' he said, still gazing into her eyes. 'I have to say I'm impressed that you only fainted – I puked all over the shop when Indi first told me.'

India clicked her tongue as she obviously remembered the moment he was referring to; she gathered her long skirts and stood up, clearing the disgusting cup of God-knows-what as she went.

He stretched his arm out towards Amber and for a brief moment she thought he was going to hold her hand. Instead he showed her a tan-coloured rope wristband.

'It's a protection talisman,' he told her, twirling it around for her to see. 'Indi made it for me when I first moved here after my parents were killed, and after she told me the town's secret. I never take it off; it's a bit like mosquito repellent.'

Amber laughed. 'It's beautiful.'

It was really pretty and not out of place on a boy's wrist. The thin rope wound around a row of haematite crystals and when Connor lifted it to her face she could smell bergamot.

'I'll make one for you and Tom after we close.'

'Why do I need one?' Amber looked confused. 'If they only take boys.'

'You've actually seen a Guardian, Amber, I'm afraid I don't know if that puts you in any danger so I'd rather you had some sort of protection, even if it's only a warning alarm that alerts you to otherworldly creatures.'

'Okay,' she mumbled, slightly alarmed at the thought of getting close enough to otherworldly creatures to activate such a thing.

'We must stay vigilant,' India was saying. 'You all must stay as far away from the church grounds as possible. If the Guardians are recruiting then that's the only soil they can walk on in our realm.'

Chapter 3

Connor was sprawled on the floor with his back to the storeroom door, a heavy book between his outstretched legs; he was studying a graphic picture of torture à la Guardian when Amber seated herself next to him.

'That's disgusting,' she said, leaning across him to look at the full colour picture. It showed a young boy, his face twisted in fear, pinned to the floor by one of the leather-clad Guardians. He was crouched over the boy's body pressing a thin blade through his heart.

'That's the Guardian ritual,' Connor said, lifting the book up to give Amber a better look. He raised his knees and brushed his thigh against hers. Amber felt her face grow hotter. She allowed her long curls to hang forward, masking her reaction as Connor pointed at the weapon used to pierce the heart.

'It's a special Guardian tool,' he said, his voice quiet as he traced a finger across the picture. 'The handle holds a deadly blood magic and when the thin blade is stuck into the heart, the liquid pumps through the victim rendering him paralysed and usually unconscious – one easy package ready for transportation to Phelan.'

Amber flinched and inhaled sharply to settle her churning stomach, a sure sign she was heading for another fainting fit or was likely to vomit in Connor's lap. He flipped the page of the book to show a series of pictures depicting the transformation process to become a Guardian. 'Once they arrive in Phelan their human blood is drained away and Guardian blood is pumped in, stripping away all their human memories. The ceremony involves many magic rituals but we have no records of those.'

'So that's what happens to the boys from our town?'

'If the Guardians take them, then yes.' He smiled ruefully as he lifted his gaze to look at her. His eyes were liquid pools of chocolate, and as she lost herself in the rugged beauty of his face she felt a sense of calm wash over her. She wondered what it would feel like to kiss him. Connor's soft voice dragged her from her thoughts as he continued, 'they probably won't remember any of it: the pain or the transformation. As far as I can gather, the blood magic makes it possible for the recruit to travel through the gateway before they are fully transformed, and they are most likely unconscious.'

'I've been thinking,' India interrupted. 'Beheading a victim is not a characteristic of the Guardians. They only take a recruit if there are no witnesses. I've heard of Guardians being disturbed halfway through a ritual and disappearing in a cloud of fog, leaving the recruit half-dead, but they never behead people, and they never target females.'

She reached for another dusty book and added it to the growing pile on the small coffee table. 'The same old legends keep coming up,' she said, pulling a large volume onto her lap, 'Guardians recruit three boys. The incident with your friend sounds like the work of a cold-blooded *human* killer, unless we can find proof to the contrary.'

They grew silent as they all pored over the books on Guardians and demons, looking for headless rituals. Amber and Tom worked through the town history books – the alternative history that neither of them had been taught in school. Amber's head began to swim again, and she was just about to suggest a coffee break when Tom leapt from his seat clutching a tattered velvet book.

'Dragovax demon!' He was practically hopping up and down as he waved the book over his head.

India took it from him and studied the open page. 'Well there's our proof.'

They all gathered closer to get a better look. A picture of a huge creature filled the page; it was dark grey with thick black veins running just under its skin. Amber's gaze strayed to the long fingers with razor-sharp talons on the end of its long muscled arms.

'The Dragovax are native to Phelan, these are the demons that are killed and imprisoned by the Guardians. This confirms it, neither a Guardian nor human killed your friend, the Dragovax did.'

'But the town pact was put in place so that Guardians prevented the demons from wandering our streets.'

'Yes, yes that's true. I've never read of a demon ever getting past the Guardian defences, unless...'

'Unless what?'

'We know the Guardians are recruiting, we believe they have their first young man. This means they are distracted. It's possible that a necromancer is using this to their advantage.'

'A necro-what?' It was Tom who asked the question much to Amber's relief. She was having difficulty holding it together with the little she did know, without adding any more supernatural beings into the mix.

India picked up a red paperback and handed it to Tom. 'Necromancers are evil practitioners who work with very black magic. They perform dark rituals of suffering, but they also have the ability to animate the dead and create undead servants.'

Tom's eyes grew wide as he turned the pages of the book.

'The demons aren't dead though, they are only imprisoned.' Amber had remembered that much from her earlier evil history lesson.

India nodded. 'True, but the passage from Phelan to the cells puts the demons in a comatose state similar to a human death. The necromancers have discovered that their unique skills can raise these demons. They just have to get past the Guardians, which has never been possible in the past. If a Dragovax escaped then its natural instinct would have been to kill first and ask questions later.' India pressed her fingertips against her temples as she spoke. 'But the only way this creature could escape is with the help of a necromancer.'

Connor picked up where India left off. 'It looks like the Guardian was hunting for a new recruit and came across the demon after he had beheaded your friend, which means the boyfriend became recruit number one.'

India shrugged her delicate shoulders. 'As awful as this situation is, we don't think there will be any more deaths by decapitation. It looks like the demon's release was only fleeting.'

Amber pinched the bridge of her nose. 'So the demon escaped, it killed Kelly and the Guardian killed the demon and then took Dan off to Guardian world. Is that everything?'

'Pretty much.' Connor shifted his position to face Amber. 'The only drawback is that the Guardians recruit three at a time and as far as we know, your friend Dan is only recruit number one. There will be two more disappearances before we can sleep easy.'

There was a loud bang on the shop door which made everyone jump. India opened the door and, after a brief exchange, she let the visitor enter.

'Dad!' Amber walked in front of the demonology books before her father could see them. 'What are you doing here?'

'I was going to ask you the same question, young lady.' He ran his fingers through his hair, nervously glancing around the shop, eyeing up the small group. 'I've been looking everywhere for you, I was worried and the coffee shop was closed.'

Amber felt a sudden pang of guilt over their recent arguments. Her dad looked so tired and she hadn't made it easy on him. There were dark circles beneath his eyes and his hair looked slightly greyer than it had the previous week. He fumbled with his car keys and shifted from one foot to the other. He looked uncomfortable in their company, which was unusual as he had always been such a people person. She wanted her old dad back, not the pathetic man that stood in front of them.

'India invited us to stay here after…after the trouble at the cemetery.' She pointed over to India who nodded her head in greeting. Her father's tight lips attempted a smile but he gave up and met Amber's gaze with a vacant expression, his eyes sweeping around the shop and over her friends.

'I'm waving a white flag,' he said raising his hand to mimic the action. 'I want us to have a family dinner tonight.'

Amber was always apprehensive when her dad suggested a family dinner. They rarely sat together anymore, and she always made up some excuse to be out at mealtimes. Making small talk with Patricia wasn't her idea of a good time.

'Tom can come too,' her dad continued, looking briefly in Tom's direction. 'It was Patricia's idea. She said you two would be upset after what happened to your school friend and we should talk about it.'

Alarm bells were ringing in Amber's head, but before she could graciously decline, Tom was shaking her dad's hand. 'Great, Mr N, we'll be there at seven.'

Her dad backed away quietly, anxiously glancing around the store until he made it to the door. He mumbled a thank you to India and left.

Amber turned around slowly. 'What the hell was that?'

'Oh come on, cutie, you know I can't resist food let alone the opportunity to wind up Plastic Patsy, it'll be fun…honest.'

She rolled her eyes and threw up her arms in a gesture of defeat then noticed the peculiar look that India was giving her.

'What is it?'

'Your dad…' She fiddled with her necklace as she spoke. 'What does he do for a living?'

'He's in sales and marketing.'

India's brow furrowed as she exchanged a strange look with Connor, who remained unreadable. After the longest pause he smiled. 'He seems great.'

She nodded and wondered if they had picked up on the whole neurotic-dad-bad-daughter vibe. She vowed to try a little bit harder to get along with him.

WHEN THEY walked through the door of Amber's house that evening, they were hit with an amazing array of sounds and smells.

Coldplay filled the house, the beats pumping out of the stereo in the living room, and the whole house smelt of home-made pizza and garlic dough balls.

'Ten out of ten for presentation,' Tom whispered, as he dug Amber in the ribs.

Patricia appeared in the kitchen doorway, her bleached blonde hair piled high in a ponytail making her look like a schoolgirl at sports day. She wore her trademark Juicy Couture tracksuit and a pair of white leather Chanel trainers.

'Just in time.' She smiled at the pair and ushered them through to the dining room.

Amber had never seen so much food; the table cloth – white of course – was covered with three varieties of pizza, an array of salads and vegetable kebabs. Her dad sat at the head of the table with a satisfied smile on his face. She thought how much brighter he looked compared to earlier that day.

'This looks great, Mr N.' Tom grabbed a chair and reached for a plate. 'Patsy, this must have taken you all day.'

Patricia visibly convulsed. 'It's Patricia,' she snapped, 'and yes it took me all day, but I'm sure you both appreciate the hard work.' Her face relaxed and her tone softened as she handed out the plates. 'We just wanted to make sure you were okay after such a shock.'

They ate in relative silence for a while, Amber finally feeling guilty enough to make a comment. 'This is lovely, thank you.'

Patricia beamed and with a tiny wave of her perfectly manicured hand she said, 'Oh it was nothing.'

Slowly the conversation began to flow, and before Amber knew it she was telling her dad all about the body at the cemetery.

Alan spoke between mouthfuls. 'It's such a dreadful shame, her parents must be heartbroken, is there any news on the boyfriend?'

Amber and Tom exchanged looks, but she shook her head. Now wasn't the time to tell her dad about Hills Heath's alternative history. 'It's not looking good for him. The police think that it could have been a lovers' tiff.'

'I'm sure he'll turn up soon enough,' Patricia said as she began to clear the empty plates. 'Boys that age are always getting themselves into trouble.' She winked at Tom and he recoiled. 'He probably didn't have such a beautiful charm bracelet to protect him.' She ran her finger along Tom's forearm, stopping at the talisman India had made for him. 'So pretty.'

'Thanks, it was a gift from India Saks.'

'Aaah, a special gift indeed if the resident witch made it for you.' Patricia chuckled as she weaved around the table clearing dishes. 'Not that we believe in that rubbish in this house, eh, Amber?'

Amber shook her head. 'Life would be so dull if we all believed in the same things.' She brushed her fingers along her own talisman as she tucked it under the sleeve of her shirt. She certainly wasn't about to confide in this woman that her beliefs had been tested today.

The conversation steered to schooldays and they began to reminisce about Kelly and Dan's school life as Patricia tidied up around them.

'Can I smell apple crumble?' Tom shouted through the open door.

A voice drifted back from the kitchen, 'Yes, I heard it was your favourite.'

Tom grinned and jumped up from the table to follow the delicious smell of baked apples and cinnamon emanating from the kitchen and permeating the entire house.

As her dad cleared his voice to speak, Tom burst through the door.

'Just popping to the shop. Pats…Patricia has run out of custard and you know how I am with my puddings.' He laughed, but Amber frowned at him.

'The shop's right by the church, it probably isn't the safest place to go.' She looked pointedly at Tom but he dismissed her with a wave.

'Patricia said it's probably THE safest place to be with all the police around. I'll be fine, cutie, I've got my protection.' He wiggled the talisman India had made for him at Amber, then pushed it under his jumper. 'Don't eat all the crumble before I get back.' With that he bolted out of the front door and into the night.

Amber did worry though. She couldn't help it. India's warning repeated over and over in her head. *'Stay away from the church.'* She hadn't thought the police made it any safer, maybe because it was an otherworldly creature they were dealing with and not a lovers' quarrel. She was pretty sure the police department didn't have a crack team of demon hunters on staff.

Her dad broke her concentration as he shuffled in his seat. 'How are you enjoying your summer so far?'

Amber looked over at her dad incredulously. The summer holidays had only just started and he knew that she had chosen to take as many shifts at the coffee shop as she could. Did he not realise it was so she didn't have to stay in the house with them?

She wondered again when they had drifted so far apart; she missed him. She missed his smile and his funny stories and she missed hearing him laugh. He seemed to be besotted with Patricia but over the past ten years she hadn't seen him relax or laugh. He was like a robot in denims and a flannel shirt.

Her phone vibrated in her pocket, allowing her a reprieve from answering her dad's question.

> [No custard at shop, feeling a bit under the weather so going home. T.]

Using this as her cue to leave, she excused herself from the table and went to bed; it had been a draining day both physically and emotionally. She replied to Tom's message telling him she'd call round in the morning, then she crawled under the covers and drifted straight off into an uneasy sleep.

THE RED-EYED *Guardian stood outside her house, watching the door with his curved blades drawn, each one dripping with blood. The front door of the house opened, and Tom walked down the path to the street. She was shouting from the window and banging on the glass with her fists, but as Tom turned to look back at her the Guardian thrust his blade into Tom's stomach and grinned up at Amber as her best friend crumpled in a heap at his feet.*

Chapter 4

When Amber crawled out of bed she felt like her head was full of cotton wool. The dreams she was having were getting more and more realistic, and it was draining her energy. Her eyes were swollen and puffy, and she realised she had been crying in her sleep.

Grabbing her phone, she sent Tom a quick message to see if he was feeling better, then jumped in the shower.

Once she was ready, she managed to escape the house unseen. She had uncharacteristically enjoyed herself last night, but she wasn't ready for full-on family bonding over breakfast too.

***

TOM'S HOUSE was all quiet when she rang the bell. His parents weren't hands-on with his upbringing and had left him to fend for himself since he was about eight. It was no surprise to find them out so early in the morning. What was surprising was that Tom didn't seem to be home either. As a typical sixteen-year-old he could always be counted on to lounge in bed until well past lunch.

She sent another message telling him to meet her at the magic shop when he dragged himself out of bed.

India was dressed in a long green velvet dress when she opened the door for Amber, her long hair was braided down her back and interwoven with green ribbon, and Amber thought she looked like an extra from a Robin Hood movie. Her smile didn't reach her eyes though, and she had faint bruises showing a lack of sleep.

Connor was stretched out on the floor, surrounded by books and parchments; he gave Amber a warm smile as she set her rucksack down beside him.

'Have you guys been to bed at all?'

Connor was still in his dark jeans and navy T-shirt from the previous day, his dark hair was slightly unkempt in a sexy kind of way, and he had a faraway look in his eyes that told Amber he could nod off at any moment.

'Nah,' he said, rolling over onto his back. 'Sleep is for the weak, and this warrior is primed and ready for action.' He yawned and stretched his arms above his head.

'Warrior!' Amber laughed loudly. 'If you don't mind me saying, you certainly don't look ready for action, you look ready for bed!'

Connor winked. 'Is that an invitation?'

Amber's cheeks turned crimson as he laughed and pulled himself up to a sitting position. She flopped down next to him, ignoring the heat running through her veins, and reached for a book.

'How was the family dinner?'

'Better than expected. Tom wasn't feeling so great though, so he went home early, but I haven't heard from him today.'

She felt the atmosphere change around her and glanced up to catch India looking pointedly at Connor with an unreadable expression.

'What is it? That's the second time in two days you've both looked like that when I've mentioned anything to do with my family, and it's freaking me out.'

'Sorry, Amber, I didn't mean to worry you, it's nothing honestly. I just sensed…great sorrow from your dad yesterday.'

Amber was shocked. She'd never associated sorrow with her dad, and he had always just got on with things in his matter-of-fact way. Miserable, moody and argumentative yes, but not sad.

'How old is your dad?'

'He's forty-two.'

'Where's your mum?'

'She walked out on us when I was six. Why?'

'Just curious.' India fiddled with the hem of her velvet dress.

'If I didn't know better, Indi, I'd say you were crushing on my dad.' She laughed out loud and was relieved that they both joined in, the oppressive atmosphere lifting slightly.

'Well, he is hot,' said India, winking at Amber as she stood.

'Ugh, that's just wrong, old people romance is never a fun topic.' She and Connor laughed as India made a mock-insulted noise at being referred to as old.

The little bell chimed as the shop door swung open. A stout figure stood framed in the doorway, her auburn hair hanging in an uncombed mass of curls. Her face was rounded with a smattering of freckles across the bridge of her nose. Amber recognised her and stood up to dust off her jeans. 'Hi, Mrs Cassidy, how are you?'

Mrs Cassidy had twins in Amber's year at school, although they were much thinner versions of their parents.

'Have you seen Carl?' She walked further into the shop and Amber noticed she'd been crying. Her face was red and blotchy, and she clutched a small handkerchief in her plump fingers.

'He went out with Cleo last night and they got separated. Cleo looked everywhere but couldn't find him so she came home on her own. Carl still hasn't come home.' She rushed over her words as they fell as fast as her tears. 'I'm sorry, I can't seem to stop crying, silly old fool, eh? It's just not like Carl to leave Cleo on her own and vanish like this.'

Amber wrapped an arm around her ample shoulders and steered her towards the open front door.

'I haven't seen him, Mrs Cassidy, but if I do I will get him to call home straightaway. I'll ask around and see if anyone else has spotted him. He'll show up soon.'

Mrs Cassidy looked up at Amber through watery eyes and smiled. She nodded her thanks and walked off down the street, stopping the first person she came across, obviously asking them the same questions.

Amber's eyes were shining with unshed tears when she slowly turned to face India and Connor; they both shook their heads.

'Please step forward, recruit number two,' Connor said, his voice barely audible.

'This is too hard,' Amber shouted. 'These are people I know, India, not just unknown faces that I read about in the newspaper.'

India wrapped her arms around Amber's shoulders and hugged her tightly.

'I know it's difficult to accept, but this pact has held for hundreds of years, it's in place to keep the rest of the human realm safe. If the Guardians didn't take their quota, then the demons could roam free and it would be a slaughter.'

Amber broke down on India's shoulder. 'I know, I do understand but I don't have to like it. These are my friends that are being taken, isn't there another way?'

India sighed deeply. 'I wish there was. As the coven leader it falls to me to ensure the pact is honoured as my ancestors did before me, but when Connor's parents died and he came to live with me, I began to question the pact myself. Connor is sixteen and can be targeted by the Guardians that I am supposed to assist…'

Amber pulled away. 'What do you mean…assist?'

India's eyes clouded over, and she looked at the floor, a cloak of shame hanging over her head.

'The Guardians can turn up at any time to claim their recruits. Once they make their presence known…I am instructed to cast a spell over the town which would draw out these young men.'

'Why the hell didn't you tell *me* that?' Connor stood up abruptly. 'That spell would have affected me this year.'

India nodded. 'I know…that's why I didn't cast the spell.'

Connor and Amber looked at each other, confusion etched on both their faces. How was it possible that India's role as coven leader was to work *with* these barbarians?

'If you didn't cast the spell then how are they recruiting these boys?'

'I honestly don't know. I think your friend Dan was a simple accident, but now this boy Carl has disappeared…I don't know how they are being drawn out and guided to the churchyard, but I know for a fact it isn't by my hand.'

Connor ran his hands through his hair as he paced up and down the shop. 'They have two recruits already, they can't both have been accidents. Nobody goes near that church if they can help it, especially now, after the headless body incident.'

'Could someone else be drawing out the boys?'

India leant down and grabbing a small book from the coffee table, flicked through it until she found the page she wanted. The colour drained from her face.

'Necromancers have a similar ability. They can draw out a demon or an undead spirit, so it's possible that they would be able to use a similar spell to the one I should have worked on the town.'

Connor halted his pacing. 'Why would a necromancer want to help the Guardians? They're only interested in raising the demons for their own…oh!'

'Oh…oh what?' Amber watched as Connor's expression hardened.

'Once the Guardians have their three recruits, they leave and return to Phelan. They have to perform the ceremony to transform the boys' blood, and if they are busy in Phelan…'

'…then they aren't guarding the demons,' India finished.

Amber had to warn Tom. He needed to know how important it was to stay away from the church. She was annoyed that he hadn't been in touch.

'Why don't we drop you home and we can tell him together?'

India snatched up her car keys and made for the door. Connor followed her out into the bright sunshine and climbed into India's battered old Volkswagen Beetle.

THEY SET off down the high street, and Amber noticed the small clusters of neighbours milling around outside their front doors. Through the open window she could hear each little faction discussing the macabre goings-on at the cemetery. Amber knew that India was right about the slaughter if the demons roamed free, but seeing her local community in such a panic made her feel unsettled.

Ten minutes later they pulled up outside Amber's terraced house and stepped out. Connor uncurled himself from the back seat and hovered at the end of the path leading to Tom's house next door, like he was her own personal bodyguard.

Tom's mum answered the door, her floaty kaftan flapping in the light breeze.

'Hey, Amber, how are you?'

'Hi, Mrs Southwark, is Tom in?'

She shook her head. 'Sorry, honey, I thought he was with you. Said he was having dinner with you last night so I figured he'd stayed over. I haven't seen him all day.'

A deep chill spread through Amber. Starting at the base of her neck the trickle of icy fear flowed down the length of her spine and radiated outward down her limbs until her bones felt frozen. She bunched her hands into tight fists to stop herself from crying as she thanked Tom's mum with a forced smile, 'No problem, catch you later.'

Connor was at her side before the front door had even closed, his arm wrapped tightly around her shoulders. Amber was too shocked to even care, and when she got back to the car she felt numb.

'He's not home, it doesn't mean anything bad has happened,' India tried to comfort her. 'He's a sensible lad, Amber, and he knows the secrets of Hills Heath, he will be careful.'

'He wasn't careful though...' she snapped, '...he went past the cemetery last night to run an errand for Patricia, and I haven't seen him since then.'

India tensed and a soft cry escaped her lips. Amber followed her line of sight and felt the scream rise up in her throat.

Lying in the gutter, almost hidden from sight, was Tom's talisman. Connor scooped it up and showed the girls. The crystals were covered in dirt from the gutter and the chain was broken.

India studied the chain, wiping the grime away with her thumb. 'This was broken using magic,' she said. 'See here?'

She held the links on her outstretched palm and pointed at the break. The metal was scorched as if it had been held over a Bunsen burner for too long, and the link had been ripped in two.

'The Guardians?' Amber asked weakly.

'No, they don't have this kind of magic. Their powers are concentrated for physical prowess and brute strength, not this.'

'Necromancer!'

'Yes, it would appear so. It's the only explanation. If the Guardians have Tom, then he didn't walk willingly into their open arms; another magical force drove him there.'

'Without his talisman, he didn't stand a chance, did he?' Amber turned the charm bracelet over and over in her hands.

India folded her arms around her in a tight hug, 'I can do a locator spell at the shop, and we will find a way to get him back. Connor and I will work the spell and you can come by later after you've rested. Don't lose hope just yet, Amber.'

As she watched them drive away, she pulled her phone out of her pocket and sent a single message [I will find you].

※

PATRICIA WATCHED her stepdaughter and her friends as they gathered together at the roadside. She couldn't make out their words, but it was painfully obvious to anyone watching that Amber was distressed.

They had found something on the street, and this had been the cause of the upset. Although she couldn't see the object from her concealed spot behind the lounge curtains, she knew exactly what it was.

The three friends hugged and the velvet-clad woman with her young companion drove away. Patricia watched as Amber pulled out her phone and began pressing the keypad.

She pushed her own manicured hand deep into her pocket and closed her fingers around the object in there, her lips curling up in a cruel snarl as the object vibrated. She lifted it out and looked at the tiny screen. It read [I will find you].

Patricia twitched the curtains back again to watch Amber as she made her way up to the house.

'I very much doubt that, sweetie,' she hissed, before burying the stolen phone back in her pocket and silently moving through to the kitchen.

INDIA STARED at the three faces displayed on her Skype screen, each box showing three very different women. Hettie was a feisty red-headed witch from the Yorkshire Dales, choosing to teach her meditation classes to the smaller villages rather than promote her healing gifts in the city; her green eyes matched her aura. Softly spoken Lydia practised homeopathy from her tiny cottage in the Welsh hills where she preferred to surround herself with cats rather than people. The third was Fay, a tough witch from the Emerald Isle, who ran a cattle farm with her five brothers. They were the closest of friends and they were coven sisters.

It was India who was chosen to move to Hills Heath as the head of the coven. Her parents had been adamant that she take on the responsibility that the High Coven offered. There had been strange circumstances surrounding the disappearance of the town's former representative, whispers that her predecessor had tried to break the town's bond with the Guardians. The head of the High Coven had assured her the Guardian pact remained intact, and she would be perfectly safe so long as she cooperated with the general. Her own coven had wanted to relocate with her, solidarity in numbers, but she had promised them she would call upon them if she needed their help.

When her brother and sister-in-law had been killed, the task of raising her nephew had fallen to her too. Moving from Hills Heath had not been an option, so she raised the boy to understand his heritage and helped him to integrate into a life of witchcraft. She taught him the true history of the town and trained him to fight, as her father had done with her.

Now, the time had come to call upon her sisters for help.

'What if it can't be done?' Hettie's face filled the screen as she leant up close to the webcam. 'It's not like this situation hasn't arisen before, and look what happened there.'

'There have been hundreds of disappearances, India. The payment to the Guardians must be honoured, why must we meddle in this one?'

'It's very unorthodox,' said Fay.

India looked at the faces of her coven sisters. They were right. These rituals were ageless, but the coven had remained detached... until now.

'I understand your concerns, and believe me when I say I have lost sleep over this situation, but I can feel a great force brewing in the town.'

A heavy silence descended as each of the witches processed the information.

Hettie spoke first. 'This girl, Amber, is she a witch?'

'No, but her father is definitely of magical origin, although she doesn't seem to be aware of it.'

'Who was her mother?'

'I don't know, she left when Amber was just six, walked out on the family and never contacted either Amber or her father again.'

'So she could have been a witch and found it necessary to flee Hills Heath?'

'I guess so; it's hard for Amber to talk about, so I haven't pressed the matter.'

Fay leant in closer to her webcam, 'I think it may be time to ask Amber Noble just what she does know about her family.'

India nodded; she had known this would be a possibility ever since Amber's father had called in to the shop that day. His aura had been a dull turquoise, and she had seen the trail of magical energy rolling off him in waves, but it had also been laced with black and grey flashes, as if he wasn't really alive but a walking, talking ghost.

'**SO YOU'RE** going to teach me how to do spells?' Amber was mildly amused. Although she was now totally convinced that magic did exist, she couldn't quite help remaining isolated from it.

'I'm doing a locator spell to find Tom, and I thought it advisable to teach you a simple protection spell,' India sighed, 'and if you could take this a little more seriously I would appreciate it.'

'Sorry, Indi, it's just...well I feel like I should be out there, searching for Tom instead of learning party tricks...' She trailed off as she saw the shadows roll across India's face.

Sweeping her arms wide and levelling her palms flat, India closed her eyes and muttered something under her breath. Two balls of blue fire appeared, each one crackling with magical energy, hovering above her hands. The lights in the shop flickered, then went out, and through the shop window Amber could see the sky growing darker as storm clouds filled the air. Clapping her hands above her head India began chanting loudly. Outside, the winds picked up and it began to rain heavily. Amber watched in utter astonishment as the residents of Hills Heath began running for cover.

As quickly as it had arrived, the storm vanished, leaving the sun to shine and the shoppers to return tentatively to the streets.

India slumped slightly as she disconnected from the spell and looked directly at Amber.

'Point taken,' she mumbled as India smiled and prepared the space for their first lesson.

'Are you going to teach me how to do that?'

'No, manipulating the elements isn't normally how one would start to learn the craft.'

She opened an old velvet book, and Amber marvelled at the handwritten notes and drawings. Brightly coloured feathers were sticking out of the pages like fluffy bookmarks.

'This is my Book of Shadows,' she explained. 'It's where I record everything about my incantations, potions and talismans.'

The cover of the book was a deep purple, and each of the creamy yellow pages was etched in gold. Every page had been filled with words, pictures, pressed flowers and herbs. Amber was awestruck. As she thumbed through the pages, the book fell open on one particular spell and her attention was drawn to the title. Destiny.

'What's this one?'

'When a witch comes into her powers she doesn't know how to use them, she needs to be taught and guided by her mentor or mother.'

Amber frowned, but India carried on. 'If no such mentor exists, this spell can point the new witch in the right direction.'

'So it's like careers advice for the supernatural?'

India laughed. 'A little, we each have different strengths and powers. Finding our right path is very important.'

'Don't you just point and shoot with your blue fire fingers?'

India snorted. 'It's a little bit more technical than that. I realised I was a witch when I turned ten; my father was a witch and taught me how to feel my power in the palm of my hands. One day we were sitting around a campfire toasting marshmallows when a spark leapt from the flames and set his trouser leg alight. He was hopping around like crazy, and I just "felt" what I had to do. I guess I did point and shoot because I concentrated on the element of fire and it went out...his flaming trousers and the campfire!'

She chuckled at the memory and continued, 'My dad was so pleased with me and we realised then that my talent was elemental magic, like the fae but not so powerful.'

Amber shook her head. 'The what?'

'The fae,' she repeated. 'Faeries.'

'You have *got* to be kidding me!' Amber rose suddenly to her feet and paced back and forth, then stopped to gawk open-mouthed at India.

'Just so we're on the same page, we have Guardians from another dimension, demons who behead people, witches who mess with the weather, and now you want me to believe that the faeries at the bottom of my garden are *real*!'

'From now on, Amber, it might be easier for you to believe that everything of myth and legend is real, and then it may not keep coming as such a shock.' India shrugged her tiny shoulders. 'Just a thought.'

'Oh great...so what, the postman's a werewolf, my teachers are vampires and old Mr Parkinson from the bakery is a goblin?'

'Don't be ridiculous, Amber. Mr Parkinson is an orc, and it's so obvious when you study the shape of his head.'

Amber threw her hands in the air and started to pace again. This was too much to handle. She hadn't finished processing the fact that magic was real, and still they kept delivering fresh surprises. Faeries, orcs, demons and witches were all living in her town. The town she had called home and the same town that for hundreds of years had been a bloodbath of gigantic proportions.

'Maybe we should take a break?'

She was halfway to the door when Connor burst through with a bag of cream cakes and a tray of hot chocolate. The sight of all that whipped cream almost drained her of her anxieties – almost.

'Hey, what's up?' Connor glanced between India and Amber, sensing the atmosphere wasn't quite right.

'Oh, the usual,' Amber began, 'just having my first lesson about witches and their unique powers and how tough they can be but not as tough as, oh I don't know, *faeries!*'

Connor glanced at India and gave a nod of his head. He watched Amber continue with her mini meltdown, then he placed the drinks and cakes on the counter and stroked his hand across Amber's cheek.

She felt all the anger and confusion drain out of her and a sense of immense peace wash through her. Her shoulders sagged and the tightness in her chest lifted. As she stared up into Connor's big brown eyes she felt very sleepy all of a sudden. Just when she thought she may nod off in his arms, she saw his eyes change colour. The deep chocolate brown gave way to a bright purple, and she could see her own reflection bathed in this new colour.

'Your eyes…' she sighed.

Connor nodded and his lips curled in a gentle smile. 'I'm half fae,' he said in a hushed tone.

The air in the room seemed to whoosh out all at once and suddenly there was only Amber and Connor, and she was very aware he was touching her, the heat from his hand pressing against her face, and a stronger heat pooling deep in her gut. She raised her hand and caressed his face, her eyes never leaving his. She was falling into them, pools of liquid purple, full of warmth and …

'Okay, Connor, that's enough.' India's voice was sharp as it cut through the air, releasing Amber.

'What the hell was that?' She recoiled when she realised she was still stroking his face, embarrassed by such an intimate touch.

Connor didn't seem to mind and only dropped his hand when she moved beyond his reach.

'I have the ability to calm feelings and lessen physical pain,' he said, pulling a large slice of Victoria sponge cake from the paper bag.

'My brother, Connor's father, was a witch but his mother was fae. This union was, and still is, fairly uncommon as the resulting child can suffer from torn personalities. In Connor's case his parents brought him up to cherish both sides of his lineage: the fae wisdom and the witch power. I have been working with him to hone his skills and manage his abilities.'

Amber watched Connor as he expertly polished off his second slice of cake before scooping a mound of cream from the top of his hot chocolate.

'I thought only girls were faeries, you know, like Tinkerbell?'

Connor laughed loudly. 'I'm also part witch, so I leave my little green dress and fairy wings in my wardrobe on weekdays,' he teased.

'Funny!'

'It's taken Connor a long time to master his dual identity,' India said. 'He has had to train tirelessly and study the legends and heritage of both cultures.'

'Can you do spells like Indi?' Amber was now intrigued, her initial shock and fear wavering.

'I can only tap into my fae magic to calm someone's emotions or relieve their pain, but Indi's trying to help me find my witch power. I can fight with swords though which is pretty cool. My dad was a brave warrior and he was a champion with his sword and staff.'

Amber noticed how his eyes twinkled when he spoke about his father, the admiration clearly evident.

'You miss them.' It was a statement rather than a question and Connor nodded.

'I was only young when they were killed, but I still remember them. My father would practise his martial arts every day after work, and my mother worked as a counsellor at the local school; the kids loved her. I guess I inherited her skills for calming hysterical students.' He winked at her and she suddenly felt very shy, remembering the feel of his hands on her face.

'The purple faerie eyes do kinda give the game away though,' he added, as he offered the bag of cakes up for her.

Amber laughed and retrieved a jam doughnut, trying to avoid spilling jam down herself as she pondered her own heritage.

'Would your destiny spell work on me, Indi?'

India shook her head. 'You're human so it wouldn't do anything but fizz and pop.'

Connor looked pointedly at his aunt. 'Maybe we could try it for her, you never know, her dad may be a shape-shifter or something.'

Amber laughed. 'I wish he could be; my dad is Mr-oh-so-boring. Patricia on the other hand is definitely a coyote or something.'

There was nervous laughter from India and Connor but she dismissed it. Her dislike for Patricia was obviously a private joke that only Tom understood.

'It won't do any harm,' India said, as she reviewed the spell. 'You probably won't even feel a tingle, but we can try.'

WHEN THE hot chocolate and cakes had gone, Amber nestled herself inside the circle of salt that India said would protect her against bad energies. She was instructed to sit cross-legged, with her palms resting in her lap, facing up and her eyes closed.

'Breathe in deeply, in and out, and keep that steady rhythm as we do the spell.'

As she sat breathing deeply and trying not to giggle, she began to think about her own family. Her dad worked so hard to provide for her and Patricia, but over the past ten years he had become more and more detached from her. She loved him so much, but when he looked at her it was as if he didn't really see her. It made her heart break a little more every day.

She could picture her mum clearly. Her brown hair was cropped at the nape of her neck and her long fringe swept across her forehead with a single strip of silver hair, about an inch wide, that she tucked behind her ear. She had always joked that having kids had turned her grey, but Amber had loved how unique it made her mum. Her hazel eyes held a flicker of blue and they had sparkled whenever the two of them had talked. Amber had never understood what drove her mum away. Her dad never mentioned it, and he had wallowed in self-pity for a few weeks before meeting Patricia. Moving on for him had been much easier than it had for her; she missed her mum so much that her heart ached.

As her mind whirled through the memories of her mum, she could feel a strange pulsating in her hands and feet.

She was shuffling slightly on the spot, thinking her limbs must be going to sleep, when she was suddenly engulfed in a heavy windstorm, every inch of her skin tingled, and she felt her long hair whipping around her face.

She screwed her eyes tightly shut, her heart racing as she was battered by the winds surrounding her.

'Humans don't feel a thing.' That's what India had said.

She no longer felt the wooden floor beneath her; instead she felt an odd weightlessness. Her head was thumping and the vibration strumming through her body was intense. Her mouth was so dry, as if she hadn't had a drink for a month.

Just when she was ready to shout for India to stop, the winds ceased and she could feel the floor beneath her legs. She was shaking from head to foot, her eyes still closed and her breath coming in short, sharp gasps. Very slowly she flexed her fingers and opened her eyes.

Connor and India were crouched on the floor behind the counter. The shop looked like a tornado had passed through it, and as she looked around her she noticed the circle of salt, her protection, had been scattered.

With wobbly legs Amber stood up and looked again at the salt. The circle was gone, and instead the unmistakable shape of an eye stared back at her.

'I'm going to take a stab in the dark here and say I'm not human.'

Her friends shook their heads.

'Well that's just terrific,' she mumbled.

IT DIDN'T take long to straighten out the shop; they worked in silence as they reassembled the wands, collected the tumble stones and picked up the many books.

Finally Amber couldn't take the silence anymore. 'Is anyone going to tell me what happened?'

India took a deep breath, holding on tightly to the counter. 'As a human, that destiny spell should not have even fizzed or popped.' She glanced around the shop briefly. 'As you can see, there was more than a little fizz!'

'It felt like I was floating, and my whole body was tingling.'

'Did you see any pictures or hear voices in your head?' Connor spoke for the first time, without looking up from his sweeping brush.

'Not really, I was thinking about my mum, and I could see her face really clearly in my mind. I saw her eyes, clothes and that quirky silver strand in her hair.'

They both stopped what they were doing to stare at her in amazement. India reached below the counter and pulled out a tiny compact from her bag. She handed it to Amber and nodded for her to take a look.

Lifting the small mirror in front of her she looked at the face that peered back. Her features were the same, but her eyes looked different; the deep chocolate brown had a small fleck of white in the centre that glowed like a light bulb. The mirror couldn't fit all of her image so she moved it slightly and stopped as she caught sight of her reflection. The long dark waves still framed her face, but to the left was an inch wide strip of pure silver hair. She reached out to touch it, winding the strand around her index finger as she tried to swallow down the despair she felt clawing its way up her throat.

'I look like my mum,' she whispered, her voice breaking in a sob.

India gave her a tight hug and ushered her to the sofa. 'Who was your mother?'

'I don't know, I don't remember much.' She pulled at the silver tendril. 'I was only six when she left and Dad didn't tell me anything. I remember what she looked like, her smell and her smile, but that's pretty much it.'

Connor knelt in front of her and ran a hand over her hair; she instantly felt a sense of calm descend over her. He kept his hand cupped around her cheek, and she nestled against him, relishing the feeling.

'You are rocking some major power,' he said softly. 'It might be time to get your dad to fill you in on your family history.'

She let out a soft whimper and nodded; maybe the time had come to rebond with her dad.

Chapter 5

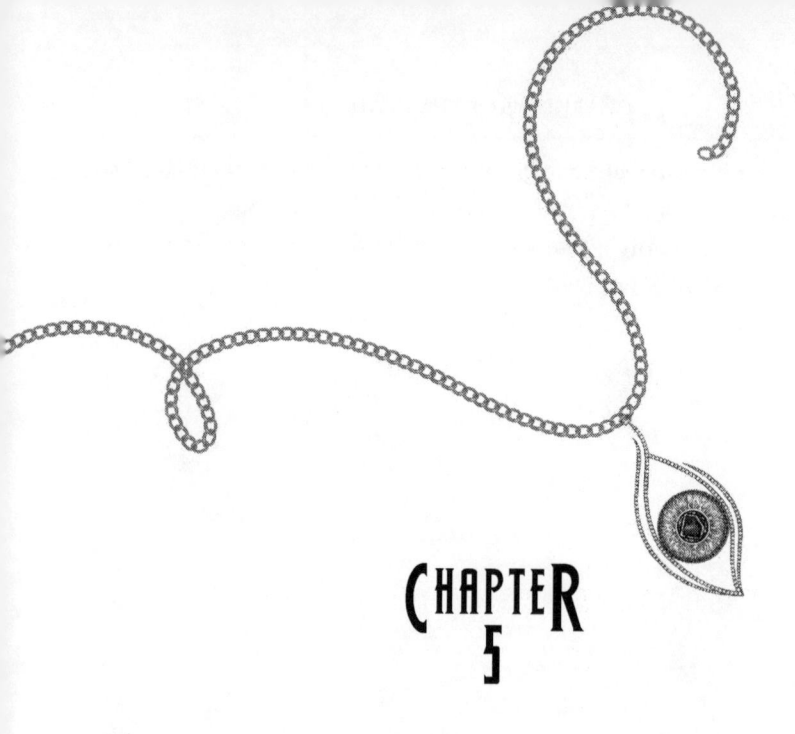

The house was empty when she got home; a note on the counter informed her that her dad had taken Patricia out for dinner and that there was leftover casserole in the fridge for her. Amber opted for an apple instead and flopped down on the nearest chair to contemplate the day.

She wasn't human. How did you start to process that kind of a bombshell? Connor had been really sweet, and once he had used his funky fae powers on her she had felt more like her old self and less like the quivering wreck she had been after the spell.

Her looks, on the other hand, were far from normal. The strip of silver in her hair fell across her eyes, and she twirled it around her finger absent-mindedly. Had her mum been a witch?

That was the only explanation India could come up with. She was going to have to ask her dad but where did she start? 'Hey, Dad, pass the salt, and by the way was Mum a witch before she dumped you and walked out? Maybe not.

Her phone vibrated and jolted her back from her daydreams [Cemetery,now! T]

Amber leapt from the chair and stared at the small screen for what seemed like an age; she'd been sending messages to Tom every hour and not heard a word, which had deepened her suspicions that he had been taken by the Guardians, but now here he was, alive and well. Her thoughts were jumbled as she worked through every scenario for his lack of contact. If he wasn't dead or dying, then she was going to kill him herself for putting her through so much trauma. She tucked her phone in her pocket and sprinted for the front door.

***

IT WAS dark as she hurried along the deserted street; ever since the beheading incident, the residents of Hills Heath had been hiding behind locked doors.

She sent a quick message to tell Connor that Tom hadn't been taken by the Guardians and had got in touch and quickened her pace.

She had missed Tom so much; they had been inseparable since they were small children, and he understood her like no-one else could. They needed each other to survive the gaping hole that their respective parents had left, and as she ran towards the cemetery wall, she realised that she didn't work without him.

The police tents had been removed from the churchyard, and it was back to being the usual creepy old graveyard she knew and loathed. His message hadn't told her specifically where to meet so she clambered over the lichen-covered wall and crouched low to avoid being spotted from the town square.

Her eyes adjusted to the gloom and she could make out the grimy headstones surrounding her. Her breathing was heavy as she wound her way through the graves. Most of the stones were crumbling from age and neglect, names and dates weathered to an illegible smear, and the whole place smelt of damp earth and death.

A movement in her peripheral vision caused her to freeze to the spot; she could feel the sweat trickling down her back as she shielded herself behind a large grey angel with its hands outstretched to the heavens.

Her heart was hammering inside her ribcage as she waited for Tom to show himself. A deep feeling of foreboding crept over her, and she mentally kicked herself for rushing into this situation without giving it any rational thought.

A sound close behind caused her blood to turn to ice; she could feel cold breath on her neck. She slowly turned to face whoever, or whatever, was standing there.

The man was tall, much taller than Amber. His hooded cape covered his head and face, his breastplate was in her line of sight and the red phoenix emblazoned across the armour sent a ripple of shock through her whole body. Its bright red features matched the red eyes she could make out beneath the hood.

'I know what you are,' she said, her voice quavering. 'I know that you are taking my friends.'

To her surprise the man chuckled, a deep throaty sound that was bereft of any humour.

He reached out and trailed his gloved finger down the side of her face, lifting her chin with his index finger so she couldn't look away.

'Amber Noble,' he said, causing Amber to squirm under his touch. How did this creature from another realm know her name?

He let go of her and grasped either side of his hood. With a flourish he tore back the cloth to reveal his face.

'Dan!' she backed away, horrified at the sight of him.

The boy she had once known was no longer a boy; his muscles had developed to reveal arms as thick as tree trunks, his solid neck met with a hard mass of chest and he looked like he had been pumped full of steroids. His head was shaved and a deep purple tattoo snaked up his neck and across his scalp, the swirls of ink moving with him as if alive, and the ink running freely beneath the skin, swirling and shifting.

His blood red eyes watched her stumble over rocks and tree roots in a feeble attempt to get away. His top lip curled up in a snarl and he moved forward with unusually stealthy grace for such a huge bulk.

Amber was trying hard not to scream. Attracting attention could land some innocent boy in a whole heap of Guardian trouble if they attempted a rescue.

'You killed Kelly,' she cried as she scrambled along the dirt.

The thing that was Dan chuckled again. 'Not me...a demon, he was punished.'

'The Dragovax?'

'Clever girl.' He stopped moving briefly and cocked his head to one side. 'Your friends are here to save you, little eye, but none of you can save him.'

Amber looked behind her to where Dan was pointing and let out a tumultuous cry. Tom lay on the ground, covered in blood from a gash to his head. His arms were limp by his sides and his glassy eyes were fixed on the night sky. Protruding from his chest was a thin dagger, buried up to its hilt in his heart. Amber could see his chest rising and falling as he struggled to breathe.

'No!' she screamed.

Dan grabbed the back of her hair and, wrenching her off the floor, tossed her to the side where she collided with a dirty stone tablet which cracked in two as she hit it. Her face smashed into the dirt and she spat the blood from her mouth. Her arm was on fire and when she tried to move it she yelled out in pain.

She watched helplessly as Dan scooped up her best friend and made his way to the church doors.

She called out to Tom, but he was unconscious, his body limp in Dan's arms.

Dan looked deep into Amber's eyes and snarled, 'We have our three – payment has been made. Until we meet again, little eye.' And then they were gone.

She could hear Connor shouting her name, and she tried to answer between her sobs, but her grief overwhelmed her and she pressed her forehead against the dirt, closing her eyes and letting the darkness take her.

AMBER FELT like she had been asleep forever. Her body ached in places she didn't know existed, but she felt a strange sense of calm. Her memories were a jumble of pictures, flames, red eyes...TOM.

Her eyes snapped open and she saw Connor sitting by her side holding her hand and stroking her hair.

'Stop it,' she snapped at him. He winced as the sting of her words hit him. Amber felt guilt drive through her.

'I'm sorry, Connor, but I need to feel.' Her voice was a low whisper. 'If I don't deal with my grief it will eat away at me.'

'I understand,' he said, leaning over her. 'I don't want to take your emotions away, I'm trying to remove your physical pain.'

He took his hands away from her, and for a minute she tried to register his words. Then the agony descended, twisting through her limbs. She winced as the searing pain shot up from her toes and seeped into every bone and every muscle. She groaned.

'You've broken your arm, two ribs and bruised your ankle.' India's voice was soft as she approached the sofa that was now a makeshift bed.

'We didn't want to take you home.' She smiled at Amber but it didn't reach her eyes, 'I wasn't sure how your dad would react.'

Amber swallowed down the scream that was threatening to surface and shook her head, stopping abruptly as even that movement caused her pain.

'I haven't had a chance to talk to him yet.' She coughed as she spoke and cringed at the hurt it caused.

'Please let me help you,' urged Connor. Amber nodded and felt the intense pain subside as he began stroking his fingers across her forehead.

'What happened?'

Amber went over the night's events in her mind, 'Tom sent me a message telling me to get to the cemetery. I didn't think, I just ran.'

TEARS ROLLED down her cheeks and Connor smoothed them away with a tender touch. 'And was he there?'

'Yes,' she nodded. 'I saw him, he was broken and the Guar... Dan!' She suddenly remembered. 'The Guardian was Dan, but not the Dan I went to school with, he was all muscles and inky tattoo and freaky red eyes. He called me *little eye* and then he took Tom. He stabbed him and then he took him.' Her whole body shook as she cried, clinging to Connor as she let all her pent-up grief out.

She eventually cried herself to sleep cocooned in Connor's arms.

She could see Tom walking down the church path. He was with her mum and they were laughing. She tried to reach them but the flames wrapped around her ankles like chains. She tried calling to them but she choked on the dry heat. They turned together and looked in her direction, their expressions blank. As she shouted out they hissed at her and then walked into the wall of flames beyond the church door. She called for them to stop. The scene shifted and she was in a garden filled with sweet-scented flowers and fruit trees. A boy stood beneath one of the trees, his long white hair glistening in the sun and his deep purple eyes twinkled as he smiled at her. She felt her heart swell as she gazed at him, his features as familiar to her as her own. She tried to cry out as a figure appeared behind him, a hooded figure with red eyes, and as the man plunged a dagger into the boy's back, she screamed.

Her eyes flew open and she took a moment to get her bearings. The shop was in darkness, and someone had covered her with a blanket as she slept. Connor was nowhere to be seen, so without his faerie magic, her aches and pains had returned, although they weren't as bad as they had been earlier.

She swung her legs off the sofa and steadied herself into a sitting position. Her head was spinning like she'd just stepped off the carousel at the funfair.

Give it a minute, she told herself as she dug her fingernails into the soft fabric.

India was fast asleep on the floor by the storeroom, wrapped in a woollen cloak and clutching her Book of Shadows.

Amber shifted on the seat, careful not to wake her. She looked at her left arm which was covered in bruises of every colour imaginable. India had said it was broken, but Amber could move it without too much pain. She lifted her leg and wiggled her ankle; she couldn't see any bruising or swelling there either.

A voice in the darkness startled her. 'You've healed yourself.'

Connor moved out of the shadows and came to sit beside her. He held yet another dusty, leather-bound book.

The front cover was intricately carved to look like an eye. Amber recognised the shape from the pattern of salt from their earlier destiny spell. Had that really only happened that morning? It felt like an eternity ago.

'Dan...the Guardian called me *little eye*,' she told Connor as he flicked through the pages. He stopped when he reached a detailed drawing that wouldn't have looked out of place in a history textbook.

There were four figures swathed in white robes. Scrolls overflowed at their feet and tumbled off the golden cloud they were sitting on. With pleading eyes, a sea of faces looked up at these figures. The images of these tormented humans were surrounded by pictures of drought, famine and death.

'Oracles,' Connor said. 'They were channels for prophecies from the gods, the authority in ancient times.'

'Why does everyone look so sad?'

'Legend has it that the oracles grew tired of people demanding their sight for profit and gain, and they fled to the four corners of the earth, leaving the world to fend for itself without a clue of what was going to happen.'

'What happened to them?'

'No-one knows, it was believed that they continued to live as humans and helped only those who showed themselves to be worthy of the sight. They integrated into human society, they married and had children.'

'And you think I could be a descendent of the oracles?'

'I know it sounds crazy, but it does make sense. You have freaky dreams, you are blatantly not human, and your broken bones have miraculously healed.'

He snapped the book shut and handed it to Amber. 'Bedtime reading perhaps.'

She traced her finger along the outline of the eye on the front cover. 'An oracle.' She spoke softly as she repeated the word. 'If that's true then why didn't I see what was going to happen to Dan and Kelly, or Tom?'

'Your powers have been cursed.' India's voice surprised them both as she uncurled herself from the makeshift bed she had created.

'Who would curse me?'

'I'm not sure yet, I'm going to contact my coven and see what we can find out.'

'If I can heal myself, does that mean you've uncursed me?'

India shook her head and in the soft light of dawn she looked older than Amber had ever seen her.

'I think that whatever was binding your powers broke when we did the destiny spell, but I also think it runs deeper. I'm not sure that the entire curse on you has been lifted, and Amber…I think the curse extends to your father too.'

'My dad? Why would you think that?'

'When I met him the other day I sensed a great magic in him, but it was grounded, like his soul has been stolen. I think both of you have been cursed and that it may have something to do with your mother leaving.'

Amber's head began to spin as she thought about the enormity of the situation. Her mum may have been in trouble and had to flee. Maybe she cursed them so they didn't follow her. Maybe whoever cursed them had killed her mum when she tried to stop them.

'You have a great amount of power inside you, Amber. Part of the curse still binds you, so your full powers are not free.'

'And just what *are* my full powers?'

Connor tapped the book in her hand. 'Time to get your study head on, it's all in the textbook and there will be a test on Monday.'

Despite herself Amber chuckled and nudged his shoulder. 'Thank you, both of you.' She smiled at India. 'I don't know what I'd do without you guys.'

'We've got your back.' Connor winked and moved off through the storeroom door.

India began to tidy up the blankets then followed Connor, leaving Amber alone with her thoughts.

Amber looked down at the oracle book in her hand. All the answers lay in these pages, Connor had said. She was about to learn the truth, maybe find out why her mum had vanished. Steeling herself, she opened the first page.

Chapter 6

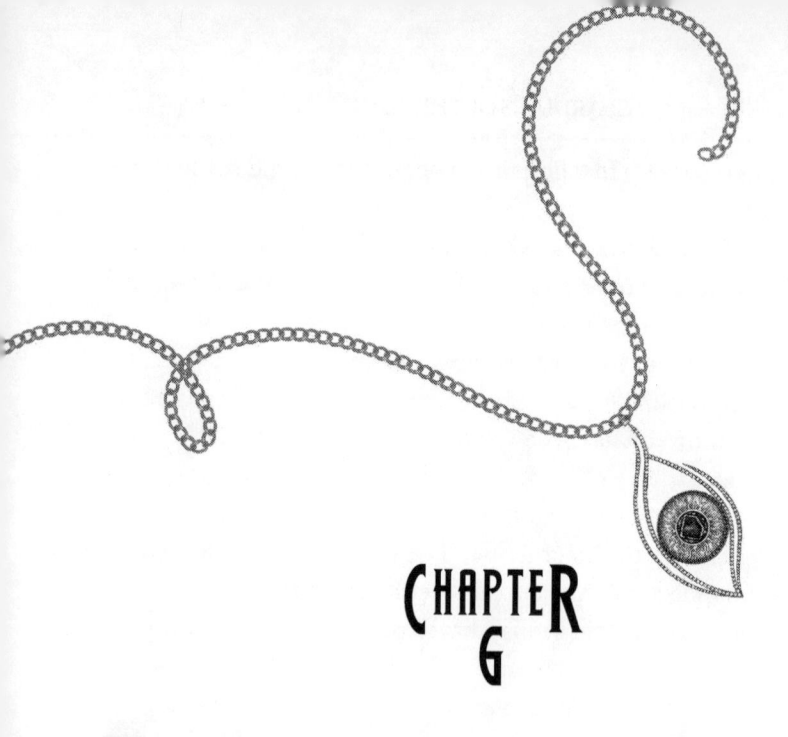

The magic shop was in utter turmoil, every square inch of floor space was taken up with rucksacks, suitcases, dusty books and bodies. India had called an emergency coven meeting, and following the recent revelations she thought a face-to-face meeting would be the better option. Amber had never seen such a diverse mix of people in one small space before, and she was starting to feel a little claustrophobic.

She had once stumbled into the girls' bathroom ahead of a school dance and had experienced the same sense of panic at being wrapped up in a fog of perfume, hairspray and pretentious airs and graces. This was similar but the fog definitely smelt more of sandalwood and lavender, and there was nothing pretentious about these women.

India was deep in conversation with the red-haired witch called Hettie. They had all breezed into the shop en masse, and the introductions had been fast.

The quiet one, Lydia, had curled up on the sofa, her silky blonde hair hanging around her face like a cloak. She was reading one of the demonology books, and when she looked up and caught Amber watching her, she smiled. Amber liked her; she wasn't quite as scary as the others. Hettie's fiery red hair made her look like she was in constant motion, the frizzy curls bouncing around her like they were alive. She reminded Amber of Medusa.

The third member of the coven was a tall witch called Fay. India had told Amber she owned a cattle farm in Ireland and she could tell Fay was a hands-on farmer when she shook her hand with enough force to rattle teeth.

'As far as we can tell there is a necromancer at work in the town. They appear to have aided the Guardians with finding their recruits and may be on the verge of raising the demons. There is every possibility that the same necromancer cursed Amber and her family.'

The four women began talking all at once, analysing their books and tossing around solutions until they were silenced by a loud crash.

All eyes turned to Amber. She was standing behind the counter holding a broken amethyst crystal, a large dent in the wooden counter showing how hard she had smashed the rock down on its surface.

'I understand that the necromancer trying to raise the demons is your priority, I know that finding that necromancer may help me with my own problems, but right now I need your help with something else.'

Fay moved to the front of the group. 'And what help is that then?'

Squaring her shoulders and setting her jaw, she took a deep breath before speaking. 'I'm going to Phelan and need your help to get me there.'

The four witches looked stunned.

'You can't,' cried India. 'The gateway is blocked by a tunnel of fire, and you'd be burnt alive.'

'When the Guardian took Dan and then Tom, they were still human when they passed through the gateway. It has to be possible to get through without the gateway key.' She knew in her heart there had to be a way to get to this other dimension and bring Tom home. 'Maybe if I could get hold of one of the Guardians' daggers I could inject myself with their blood and...'

The four women began shouting and talking at once.

'Stab yourself...are you mad?'

'Their blood is mixed with evil magic; even a drop would kill you...'

'You're not even human, we don't know what powers you have yet, and you can't go swanning off to demon realms…'

'STOP IT!' Connor stood beside Amber, his booming voice holding a tone of authority that silenced the four witches instantly. He held a scroll above his head; the yellowing paper was torn and smelt of tree bark. 'The coven can open the gateway to Phelan.'

Everyone, including Amber, stared at him with open mouths.

'This scroll tells of a coven which opened the gateway long enough for one of the members to pass through safely. They met with the general of the Guardians in reference to the pact before the gateway key was forged. It may be hundreds of years old, but I think it might work.'

He set the aged paper on the counter and the women crowded around it. There were a series of grunts, nods and a-has before India looked up at them.

'We could try it…but I'm not making any promises.'

Amber smiled.

'The coven must find a way to locate this necromancer before they raise any more demons. Now the Guardians have their sacrifice they will return to Phelan for the ceremony, and our town is vulnerable.' India shook her head as she looked up at Amber. 'Hopefully we will be able to unbind your curse at the same time, but are you sure you trust us to do this without you? We would be unable to travel to Phelan with you, you'd be on your own.'

Amber tried to keep her voice steady as she spoke, 'I understand, thank you.'

She smiled at the other witches, feeling slightly dazed. She was pretty sure she had just volunteered to travel through a wall of flames, into another dimension where beheading demons and murderous Guardians lived, to find her best friend, rescue him and get home in one piece.

Fay strode over to her and placed a calloused hand on her shoulder, 'I think we might make an oracle out of you yet, little eye.' She smiled and Amber chuckled.

'The curse on your powers shifted when you did India's destiny spell. You may find that your powers begin to unfold over time. Read up on your ancestors, this will help you to integrate the skills as they appear. We wouldn't want you turning yourself into a toad now.' She laughed loudly as she walked away.

'Could I do that?'

India laughed and shook her head, 'No, Fay is teasing you. She's right about your powers though. They will start to appear over time and you will be on your own as you learn to use them.'

Amber nodded, 'I understand, Indi, and I promise to be careful.'

The women made their way upstairs to India's apartment, their mix of accents sounding like a marching band as they jostled their bags up the tiny staircase.

India turned back to Amber and wrapped an arm around her shoulders.

'I like them,' Amber said quietly, 'your coven…they're a bit full on, but I like them.'

India chuckled. 'We have been coven sisters for over twenty years, we know what each other is thinking and feeling.' She sighed. 'They can be a bit much at times, but they're my family and I trust them with my life.'

'Do you trust them with *my* life?'

She looked down at Amber. 'We will find a way to unbind you and rid the town of this necromancer, and we will get you through to Phelan as safely as we can, but I want you to do something for me, Amber.'

'What?'

'It will take us time to prepare the spell. I want you to train with Connor, he can teach you how to tune into your energy centres which can protect you, and he will show you how to use a weapon, just in case.'

Amber felt her palms become sweaty as she thought about needing, or using, a weapon, but she gave a quick nod of her head. 'Agreed,' she said. 'I'll do my best to learn from Connor. Of course all this extra study should get me extra credit at school, you know.'

They laughed and India hugged her tightly. 'I'm so proud of you.'

'I'm verging on insanity rather than pride at the moment, but I'm sure that will change into blind panic when I set off.'

India's voice took on a more serious tone as she spoke. 'Make sure you talk to your father before you leave. He deserves to know something. I don't think he realises he has been cursed, so it may be wise to avoid telling him outright until we are able to locate the necromancer responsible. He does deserve a goodbye though.'

'Yeah, I know.' The thought of saying goodbye to her dad felt like a heavy boulder had been placed on her chest.

ONCE AGAIN the house was deserted when Amber finally got home. She packed her rucksack with spare clothes and a torch. *What exactly do you pack when travelling to a dimension of hell?*

She made herself a sandwich and as she ate she wandered through the stark white, minimalistic rooms. There was no heart to this home anymore, and Amber felt like a stranger in her own house. She opened the door to her dad's office, partly hoping he would be sitting at his desk, head bent over whatever presentation he was working on.

His woody aftershave lingered in the air, and Amber inhaled his scent, visions of family picnics and cycle rides filling her mind. Tears slid down her cheeks before she could stop them. What had happened to her family?

In such a short time she had discovered she was an oracle, that she and her dad had been cursed and that he may be supernatural too. There was every possibility that her mum had been a witch and had either been killed because of it or forced to run. She had believed that her straight-laced dad could only ever be straight-laced, not magical. That didn't fit the jeans and flannel shirt image. Her whole world was turning upside down and there was no-one she could turn to. For the first time in a very long while she really needed her dad.

She glanced down at the desk and saw a scribbled note on the pad addressed to her; *Gone away with Patricia for a mini-break, see you in a few days, Dad.*

'Oh well, that's just great,' she shouted at the empty house. 'Just when I need you, Dad. Yeah, thanks for nothing.'

She grabbed her rucksack and stormed out of the house, slamming the front door behind her.

'**BACK SO** soon?' Connor was in his usual position, spreadeagled on the floor, surrounded by books.

'Don't you do anything other than read?' she snapped as she threw her rucksack on the floor.

'Hey, grumpy, what's up?' He sat up and studied Amber as she sank to the floor.

'Dad's gone away, no goodbye, no kiss and promise of a postcard, he just went.'

'Ah, and you were hoping for a big tearful farewell before venturing into a dimension of hell.'

Amber glared at him. 'Is it too much to ask?'

'What would you have said to him? Hey, Dad, just popped in to say I'm off out for a couple of – oh I don't know, weeks, months or years to save my buddy and possibly get myself killed or turned into a lava-sucking freak?'

The anger Amber had been holding onto melted as she watched Connor mimic her 'could have been' conversation with her dad. In the end all she could do was laugh.

'Point taken, I'm just gutted I couldn't at least give him a hug.'

'Ah, yes, the human need for affection.' He wrapped his own arms around his body, hugging himself, and laughed.

'You hug Indi,' she protested.

'Indi's human, yes she's a witch but a human witch just like I'm part human on my father's side.'

'So you are part supernatural then, like me?'

'My fae side is supernatural, yes, but I don't know enough about oracles to know if you are whole or part human. I guess we'll have fun finding out on this trip though.'

'We!' Her eyes grew wide as she looked at Connor, not daring to believe what he might be implying.

'You didn't think I'd let you go on your own, did you?'

Amber launched herself at him and flinging her arms around his neck she clung to him.

'Definitely human,' he chuckled. 'Only humans can hug that tightly.'

IT WAS standing room only in the tiny living room of India's apartment. Fay and Hettie had spread their books and scrolls across the sofa and were working on deciphering the spell. Lydia was serving up one of her special herbal teas, and India was setting wards around the room to protect them as they worked.

'She's a strong one, that's for sure.'

'Yes, she is; she's taken all the news incredibly well considering how young she is.'

'We were younger than Amber when we discovered our magic.'

'Yes, but discovering magic and finding out you are an oracle, are worlds apart. She's supernatural, for heaven's sake.'

Lydia handed out her tea. 'Are you any closer to finding out who cursed her, Indi?'

'I may be; in the oracle book it tells of a man who, thousands of years ago, had his sight bound by black magic. He carried on living his life but couldn't access his powers until one day he discovered a demon and its necromancer. The demon sensed the power coming from the oracle and panicked; the necromancer couldn't hold the creature and ended up losing his head – literally. As soon as the necromancer was dead the oracle regained his full power.'

'So a necromancer does have the ability to bind an oracle's power?'

'It did in this case, but when the oracle's power returned to him, it was tainted with black magic and sent the man insane. He killed everyone in his village and then himself.'

'So how do we unbind Amber's power from the necromancer so that the same thing doesn't happen to her?'

India shook her head. 'I don't know.'

The four women grew silent and glanced around at the mountain of reference books.

'There has to be an answer in this lot somewhere.' Fay grabbed the nearest book from the floor. 'And I for one intend to find it.'

Chapter 7

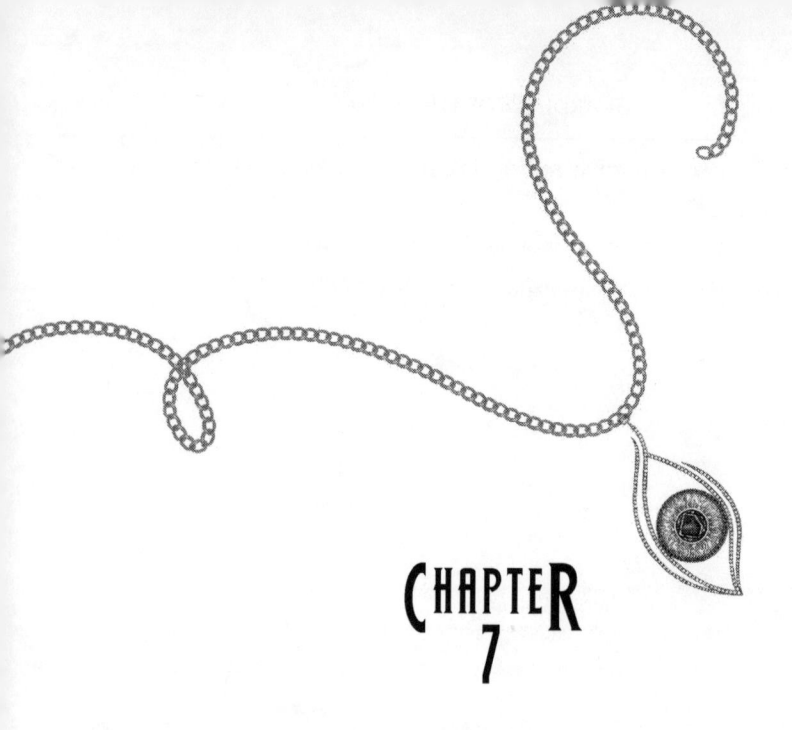

It was hard to concentrate on anything other than the fact she was alone with Connor, in a dark shop with just a flicker of candlelight for company. He had instructed her to sit cross-legged on the floor and breathe deeply; this of course wouldn't have been a problem if he wasn't sitting so close to her.

With her eyes tightly shut, her other senses were on high alert. She could smell the faint musk of his shower gel mingled with the spicy perfume of the frankincense essential oils.

Her heart was hammering inside her chest and she was convinced he would abandon their training due to the incessant noise.

'Breathe in through your nose, fill your lungs and then release softly through your mouth.'

She tried hard to do as he instructed, and before long she did start to feel a sense of peace fall over her.

'My hands are tingling,' she said uncertainly.

'Good, you might feel the same sensation in your feet too.'

She realised he was right and was surprised to feel the strange vibration running from her feet and lower legs up to her chest.

'I want you to follow my voice.'

She listened out for him and jumped when she felt his breath close to her ear.

'Picture a bright white ball of light floating above you. Watch it drop and cover you completely, surrounding you in the shining light like you are suspended inside a bubble.'

She could see the light clearly and watched in awe as her mind did as Connor had instructed. The ball of light wrapped itself around her like a cloak and her entire body quivered as it settled over her. She let out a soft gasp.

'You're doing great.'

Connor's whispered tones began to melt into the background, her stomach, which had been lurching, began to settle and her throbbing head began to feel lighter. Her breathing deepened as she felt wave after wave of profound relaxation rise up from her feet and wash over her to the top of her head. She felt all the tiny hairs on her body standing to attention.

'Picture the ball of light hovering in front of your forehead.' Connor relayed his instructions and Amber felt herself following like a willing slave. She was vaguely aware of the shop and the distant noise of life carrying on beyond the walls. Connor was sitting by her side, but at that moment she was disconnected from everything. It was an odd sensation but not totally unpleasant.

'Open up your mind and welcome the light,' he said. 'We are going to open your brow chakra and connect with its energy. Picture an eye opening in your forehead, ask to see the energies that belong beyond this realm…'

Amber could sense him talking but his words weren't registering. She was watching the huge floating eye that was sitting just beyond her reach. In her mind she stretched out a hand and pushed very gently with her fingertips until the eye split down the centre and opened like two ornate doors. The two halves shone brightly as they swung wide to reveal a field of clouds.

She took a tentative step onto the nearest cloud; it felt solid beneath her feet. When she looked down, her toes had disappeared from sight beneath the swathes of fluffy cotton wool. The space was bright, but Amber couldn't see any source of the light. It was as if the clouds themselves were illuminated.

She moved forward slowly, searching the horizon for signs of life. A voice behind her made her jump; it wasn't Connor's voice this time but that of a woman.

'Welcome, little eye.'

Amber faced the source of the voice. A tall woman with silver hair that reached the floor stood in front of her. She wore a long, plain white gown with a simple silver necklace, an ornate silver eye dangling at the end of the chain.

'Am I dreaming?'

The woman laughed and it sounded like tiny bells tinkling in a light breeze.

'You are not asleep, little eye, yet you are not awake. We exist in the space between, in your expanded consciousness. As an oracle you can access this space and link to us whenever you are in need.'

'Are you an oracle?' Amber thought she was probably stating the obvious, but she reminded herself she was new to all this supernatural stuff and waited for a reply.

'We are both oracles, my child. I am Lavanya, an ancient oracle who no longer walks your realm and you…you are a new kind of oracle, strong and powerful but with a veil over your mind.'

'What do you mean, ancient oracle?' The beautiful woman standing before her looked not much older than India.

'The ancient oracles divided their powers and moved to the four corners of the earth. We grew tired of the squabbles of humankind.'

Amber swallowed hard as she realised Lavanya was one of the ancient oracles from the book Connor had given her.

'We carried on with our lives and were lucky enough to marry and have our own children. This produced a future generation of oracles, but as each generation was born, their powers were diluted. They each had prophetic dreams or a sixth sense, some had abilities for magic or great strength, but none held all of the seven powers.'

'What powers do you have?'

Lavanya smiled and her eyes twinkled as she spoke. 'I, along with my brothers and sisters, held the seven powers until we divided, then we each took only two, together with our expanded link to one another. My powers are for healing and sight. I can see the future mapped out for everyone.'

'Wow that must take up a lot of headspace!'

'Indeed.' She laughed again. 'My brothers and sisters have the ability to lead great armies, they are skilled in combat, stealth and have great strength and elemental magic. My own magic is strong and my sight is a powerful tool, but I can only see what is mapped out. Every individual has their own ability to change any outcome.'

Amber's eyes filled with tears, and she brushed them away with her hand. Lavanya reached forward and caught a single teardrop on her finger. As Amber watched, it crystallised into a perfect diamond. She placed it into Amber's hand and pressed her palm closed.

'Nothing is impossible. Your friend is safe, little eye, but for how long depends on his own strength and your courage.'

'He's alive?' Relief rolled over Amber.

'For now, yes,' she nodded. 'But he is weak.'

'What can I do?'

'You are a rare oracle, Amber Noble, descended from two ancients. When your parents had you, they reunited the ancient powers once again, and all seven powers flow strongly within you, but you must lift the veil so you can tap into them.'

'Veil? Do you mean the curse on my family?'

'Yes, there is evil magic at work here, and you are shaded from seeing your true potential because of this veil.'

'The coven are working on it; they are trying to find a way to break the curse.'

'Concentrate, Amber, you have the power to lift this veil yourself, focus all your strength inwards.' As she spoke she pressed a long finger against Amber's forehead, right between her eyebrows. Amber felt an intense pressure build up inside her head and just when she thought her head would burst she felt a 'pop' and was blinded by a bright white light, like a million stars had exploded all around her.

She threw up her hands to shield her face.

'AMBER. ARE you okay? What the hell happened?' Connor's voice brought her back with a jolt to the small shop on the high street, full of dusty books and crystals. The smells and sounds were familiar, but Amber felt an ache in her heart that her time amongst the clouds had ended so abruptly. She had so many questions.

'Amber?' Connor was on all fours, his face mere inches from hers.

'Hi.'

'Hi! That's all you can say...hi! Bloody hell, Amber, you've been in a trance for half an hour. I couldn't wake you up and then when you finally do return to the land of the living all you can say is hi!'

She shrugged her shoulders and gave him a small smile. 'Sorry.' She rolled the word off her tongue slowly, hoping he would think she was cute instead of insane. His piercing eyes dropped to gaze at her lips and he leant in closer. Amber could feel his breath on her face.

'I was worried,' he said, his voice slightly gravelly, before he gently pressed his lips to hers.

Amber felt the heat rising up from her stomach, filling her chest and continuing to flood her cheeks. She moved her hands and ran her fingers through his thick hair, as his lips moved on hers. He shifted his position on the floor and pulled her closer to him, his strong hands circling her back and lightly stroking along her spine.

They were both breathing hard when he pulled away, and she noticed how flushed his complexion was.

Before they could speak, the door at the back of the shop opened, and the tender moment they had shared was interrupted by the rush of excited voices as India and the others burst into the room.

They leapt to their feet, dusting off their jeans and rearranging the candles. The four coven witches watched, amusement dancing in their eyes, as the two of them coughed and cleared their throats. Amber rubbed at her mouth in a bid to erase any signs of the passionate embrace they had just shared.

'So...' Connor coughed again as he ran a hand through his unkempt hair and looked India in the eye, '...what's up?'

Amber could tell that India was trying her absolute hardest not to smile and she cringed inside. Of all the times for them to walk in, it had to be then.

'We've worked out the spell for the gateway,' she said. 'We had to translate it for a modern coven but it should still work.'

'You'll have a window of about two minutes to get through the gate,' Hettie added, 'then we have to close it again so the demons don't escape.'

Amber wrinkled her brow. 'How do we get back then?'

'We understand that your priority is Tom, but as part of your mission we also need you to find the gateway key. If we have the key then the Guardians will be unable to enter our realm, freeing Hills Heath from this curse; however, if you fail to retrieve it then we can redo the spell and reopen the gateway, and you'll have another two minutes to get back across, but the Guardian pact will still exist.'

Connor nodded and studied the scroll in India's hand. 'How will you know when we are through or if we need you to reopen the gate?'

India handed him a necklace with a flat crystal pendant attached. 'Use this in the same way you would a scrying mirror,' she told him. 'Concentrate your power and connect to me through the stone. We will be able to see one another through the surface of the crystal.'

Connor looped the pendant over his head and tucked it into his shirt.

'Keep working on channelling your chakra energies with Connor.' Amber could see the sly smile playing at the corners of India's mouth as she said it. 'Your powers should start to come through slowly.'

Amber mentally kicked herself and threw her hands into the air; lost in the memory of her brief kiss with Connor she had totally forgotten about her vision.

'Lavanya! In my training session, I met a woman called Lavanya.'

The coven sisters turned as one to stare at her. 'As in the ancient oracle goddess Lavanya?'

'Yes, she told me a bunch of stuff about my heritage and about the evil power that's put a veil over my mind, but she also told me that I can lift it myself and then it's hey presto – oracle powers.'

'Did she say what powers exactly?'

'Not really, she mentioned seven powers in total and how they had split them all up when they did their vanishing act. She seems to think I have all seven hidden deep inside me.'

She gave them a lopsided smile.

India clapped her hands together and herded the others back towards the door at the back of the shop. 'Come on, come on, we all have work to do.'

Before she closed the door, she levelled her gaze at Amber. 'We open the gateway at sunrise, so you don't have long to work on your training. This is going to be a learn-on-the-go kind of mission.'

'I get it, Indi, but I do feel different somehow, like I can feel something just under my skin, an itch that I can't scratch.'

'Your powers are going to appear over time. You'll have to be very adaptable and learn to deal with each one as it emerges. Connor will help you as much as he can, but Amber...use them wisely.'

It hadn't occurred to her until that moment that her powers could be dangerous. Suddenly she wasn't so sure she wanted to be a supernatural being, however helpful it may be in finding Tom.

ONCE INDIA had left, Amber and Connor were once again alone in the dark shop; night had fallen and Connor moved to the window to lower the blinds.

'I'm sorry about earlier,' he mumbled. 'I shouldn't have kissed you like that.'

Amber flushed again in the candlelight. 'And just how *should* you have kissed me then?' she teased, but his expression turned her heart to stone as he faced her.

'I shouldn't have kissed you at all, Amber.' He paced in front of her, his face a steely mask. 'We have a dangerous mission coming up, and I shouldn't have complicated things by kissing you.'

Amber felt winded. She was used to being rejected by the men in her life, every attempt at a boyfriend had ended in disaster, and the one man she should have been able to count on, her dad, rejected her more than most, and yet Connor's rejections hurt more than any of the others.

'It's fine,' she whispered, lowering her head. 'Stressful times make people do all sorts of silly things.'

'It wasn't silly, Amber.' His voice softened and she raised her face to look at him, his brown eyes clouding over as he took a step back. 'It wasn't silly, it was stupid.'

She wasn't winded this time, she was carved in two. Her heart felt like it might implode in her chest.

'It's no problem,' she bristled. 'Dangerous mission outranks kissing – got it!'

They both stared at the wooden floor for a few moments, not speaking until Amber broke the silence. 'Better get back to my training then, we're on the clock.'

Sitting back on the floor in the centre of the protection circle, she crossed her legs. As she settled herself into a deep breathing rhythm she heard Connor finally move and take a seat beside her.

She tried hard to concentrate on the wheels of energy, balls of light and her breathing, and not on the hot tears that threatened to spill from her eyes and Connor's warm body next to hers.

Once again she could see the ball of light above her head and, at Connor's instruction, she cloaked herself in its protection then concentrated on the space between her eyebrows.

Something tugged at her mind, like she was pushing and someone was pulling from the other side. It was an odd sensation and one she wasn't taking any pleasure in, when suddenly it gave way and a violet blue light flooded her vision.

THE LIGHT *swirled and twisted, leaving trails of patterns imprinted on the back of her eyelids. As it grew brighter it began to take shape, each swirl settling in a bubble like a lava lamp. She could see small figures inside each of the violet bubbles, the figures becoming clearer until she was watching hundreds of pictures, mini home movies floating around in her mind. She concentrated on one of the bubbles and the scene unfolded.*

A young couple sitting around a kitchen table, surrounded by wedding gifts and cards. They were eating dinner and the woman was smiling up at her new husband as he refilled her wine glass. The picture shift-

ed and Amber could see the woman huddled on the floor, weeping, her husband looming over her and shouting; another shift and there was an ambulance outside and the young woman's body was being taken from the house covered in a black zip-up sack, the husband now sitting in the back of a police car.

The bubble popped and another scene drifted into focus; this time there was a man and his daughter, crying. Amber felt sad as she watched the two lonely figures nestled together in a grief-stricken embrace. As she watched, she saw a heavy black fog float down over them, seeping into their noses and mouths and settling on their clothing. The figures stopped crying and the scene shifted; a young girl approached the gates of a school, her dad waving at her as she walked across the playground. There was a woman standing behind the man, holding his hand and watching the young girl like a falcon watches its prey. Amber felt the panic squeezing the air from her lungs as she realised what she was seeing. This was no vision, this was her own memory, and as she studied the woman she saw the blonde hair fade to grey and the designer clothing turn to rags, the perfectly manicured hands twist into claws and her skin shrivel until her eyes were sunken pools of blackness in a wizened face. And then it was gone, the veil was gone, and she remembered – she knew – Patricia wasn't what she seemed. The woman who had been a part of her life for the past ten years, who had made her life a living hell, had cursed Amber and her dad.

Amber's screams echoed through the tiny shop as the enormity of it hit her. Patricia was the necromancer.

Chapter 8

The temperature was cool as the sun began its ascent from behind the imposing structure of the old church. The thick, sandstone walls cloaked any hope of feeling the early morning warmth, and the chill in the air caused goose pimples to cover Amber's arms.

She had tried repeatedly to call her dad but his phone was switched off. She'd even tried to call Patricia, but again she got no answer. India had asked if she wanted to abandon the mission to rescue Tom and concentrate on finding her father. She had felt so torn. She loved her father and knew she had to find a way to free him from the necromancer's curse but she knew she couldn't leave Tom to the fate that awaited him. If Patricia had kept them both under her curse for ten years she obviously had long-term plans, and that gave Amber some time.

India assured her the coven would handle the situation in her absence and that once the two of them had cleared the gateway they would put all their efforts into finding Alan.

As Amber and Connor made their way through the graveyard, she cast her mind back to the vision she had seen as her brow chakra opened and the veil unravelled. She had always disliked Patricia, but now she felt more than mere dislike. It was a heavy ache that lay deep in her gut, like a disease that had invaded her very bones. It was pure hatred.

Her mind was a jumble of thoughts and memories; pictures that had been hidden from her by the veil of dark magic tumbled forward and she was having a tough time controlling them all. She hadn't told India, or Connor. This was her burden to carry.

She remembered her mum more vividly now and realised that she would never have left them. Something had happened to her and Patricia was probably the reason.

She could trace the trail of dark magic in her mind, following it like breadcrumbs until she found all the hidden memories: her mum's disappearance, her dad's strange and erratic behaviour and his hostility towards her, his sudden acceptance of another woman, her miserable existence and feeling like an intruder in her own home, and then of course there was Tom. Patricia had used the dark magic to ensure Tom was at the church when the Guardian came to claim his payment; she had ripped his protection talisman from his wrist using her evil magic and as good as delivered him to the gates of Phelan herself.

Payback was going to be a bitch when she got home – *if* she got home.

Connor placed his rucksack at her feet and secured a dagger inside his heavy boot. India had insisted they both dress in black so they could blend in with the landscape in Phelan. Connor wore a pair of black combat trousers with pockets squirrelled away in every fold of fabric. He had expertly filled each pocket with weapons and food. Apparently practicality came before fashion on this trip.

Amber had quietly sneaked out of the shop to retrieve some clothes from home. She dug out a clean pair of black jeans and a black blouse and pulled on her trusty Converse and one of Tom's black zip-up hoodies she found under her bed.

'You ready?' Connor secured his rucksack onto his back and looked over at Amber, his eyes glowing purple in the twilight, showing her he was already using his fae protection magic.

'I'm as ready as I'll ever be.' She smiled and swung her own rucksack over her shoulder.

THEY MOVED as one through the graves, the aged stones protruding from the earth like decaying teeth in a dragon's mouth.

The solid church doors loomed ahead of them as they silently approached. Amber ran her hand along the ornately decorated surface, remembering all the people she had lost in her dreams once they passed through these doors. Connor turned the wrought-iron handle and pushed his shoulder against the wood. It creaked open and they stepped through into the dank interior of the church.

She was surprised to find the interior had retained its church-like qualities. To her left were rows of wooden pews covered in cobwebs and grime. They faced a stone altar, raised on a plinth, with a dark stone table at the centre. To her right was the baptistery, a circular font made of the same grey stone; it stood empty.

'This way.' Connor gestured for her to follow him into the darkness

They made their way to the far wall of the church where another door stood ajar; Connor grabbed a torch from one of his many pockets and pointed it at the black void beyond the door.

'This is the start of the staircase,' he said. 'We have to go down quite deep to find the gateway. Hold the rail and you should be okay.'

Amber peered into the darkness and her skin began to crawl like a hundred ants were racing up and down her limbs. With her eyes fixed on the gloom beyond the door, she stepped forward.

THE STAIRCASE was a rickety metal frame set into a round turret at the back of the church; it smelt of rust and decay. The stairs spiralled down into the inky blackness, and Amber's hands trembled as she clung to the cold metal railing. Their boots vibrated on each step as they descended, leaving a musical trail in their wake.

The lower they went the more oppressive the air became. Amber hadn't suffered from claustrophobia before, but she was fairly certain this was what it must feel like. Her lungs were tight in her chest and her throat felt like it was closing in on itself. She curled her fingers around the rail and steadied herself.

'You okay?' Connor's voice floated up from several steps below.

'Just feeling a bit overwhelmed, I'll be okay in a minute.'

'It shouldn't be much longer,' he said.

She began moving again, keeping her eyes on the faint silhouette of the stairs in the dim light from Connor's torch. Her head was spinning from the ever decreasing spiral and just when she thought she might actually throw up, she noticed the space around them growing lighter, not the pale light from Connor's torch but an eerie green light which filled Amber with the first trickle of fear.

'Be careful, the staircase ends here.' Connor held out a hand to support her as she jumped off the last step.

'Thank goodness,' she gasped and stepped out onto a metal platform.

They were in some sort of cage, the walls and ceilings made of interwoven metal, and it reminded her of the chain-link fences that surrounded the kids' play park by her house. Metal sconces with black candles hung from the intricate barrier, the flames sparking with a ghostly green glow. Amber could make out a large door to her right, but as her eyes adjusted to the murkiness, she was transfixed by the view beyond the cage. She walked to the nearest fence and looked through the wire, lacing her fingers through. The cage was supported by solid rock and was halfway down a huge circular cavern carved within the earth. As her eyes travelled down the rock face, she could see hundreds of doorways chiselled out of the stone, each hole barred with a heavy wooden door and each door marked with a phoenix symbol painted in red. The cell doors filled every inch of the cavern walls above and beneath her, thousands of them spreading deep into the black hole below. Her stomach lurched at the sight. Demon cells.

'This way.' Connor moved off to the right and pushed on the door embedded in the black rock. It screeched in protest as he inched it open. Drawing a thin dagger from his belt he slipped through the opening.

The network of tunnels ran like a maze through the rock, a deterrent for any demon who escaped, according to Connor and his books.

'They may escape through the doors but with this many tunnels it would take them forever to navigate their way out. Apparently they aren't very bright.'

'That's all very well, but how are *we* supposed to find our way?'

He smirked in the gloom and lifted a milky-coloured crystal above his head; it shone brightly as if powered by electricity and then floated off down one of the tunnels.

'Indi worked her mojo on some of the crystals and voilá, we have our very own tour guide.'

She laughed. 'That's pretty cool.'

Their 'tour guide' took them through the maze of tunnels until eventually the air began to close in around them and the walls grew too hot to touch.

'I'm guessing our wall of fire is getting close,' Connor mumbled as he stripped out of his jacket.

The wall of fire turned out to be an entire tunnel of fire and molten lava. The walls were alive with flames, and the stone floor glowed blue like the very centre of the flame of a match.

'There is no way India's spell will drop all of that long enough for us to make it through.' Amber stared at the impenetrable tunnel.

'She said the spell will work. We just have to trust her.'

Using the pendant India had given him, he circled his palm around it and chanted softly, the deep purple turning milky-white then becoming crystal clear. In the centre of the crystal Amber could make out India's face.

'We're here,' Connor spoke to the crystal, and Amber could hear India's disembodied voice respond, drifting out of the stone itself.

'We are ready too. You will only have a few minutes to make it through. When the flames drop you must move quickly.' She laughed nervously and added, 'Fay has read that the gateway is guarded but we don't know by what. Be on your guard, Connor.'

She wished them luck then returned to the coven.

The stone continued to glow.

'Can she still hear us?'

'No, it will stop glowing when we are safely on the other side, and the twin crystal in India's possession will do the same so they know we made it through.'

'Right then.' She faced the wall of flames. 'Ready or not, here we go.'

THE DOOR at the back of the shop led to the storeroom; dusty packing boxes lined the walls and a heavy, mahogany shelving unit housed a selection of jars in varying shapes and sizes. In the centre of the room, marked out on the wooden floor, was a pentagram. It was painted in a deep red and shimmered in the soft candlelight. Wisps of sandalwood smoke filled the room as India ushered the women through and closed the door behind her.

As she looked at her coven she could see the blue sparks of magical energy caressing their auras.

'Ladies, if you please.' She swept an arm over the symbol and they took up their positions.

India trailed a circle of salt around them, forming the protective barrier.

'It's time.'

She nodded at each woman in turn, and they joined hands, chanting softly as the candle flames danced around them. In the centre of the circle the air began to shimmer and crackle with blue fire, and the air twisted as it fought against itself.

The candle flames shot towards the ceiling, illuminating the coven, and beads of sweat glistened on the forehead of each member as they concentrated on the spell at hand. India could sense the power coursing through her veins, the tickling vibration of electricity as it flowed from witch to witch, from sister to sister, building in power as it circled the coven. The soles of her feet were burning as the magic pulled its energy from the earth.

The air within the circle tore apart and a hurricane filled the small space, ricocheting off the women as they stood rooted to the spot, firmly holding each other's hands.

'We invoke the goddess to open the gateway and allow safe passage for our friends,' India shouted into the storm.

The winds grew more ferocious, and India could faintly see the flaming tunnel within the circle.

'It's working,' she shouted.

The air around them became sticky with heat, and an oppressive atmosphere settled over the coven. The image of the gateway shuddered within the circle before receding out of sight. In its place stood a huge phoenix; flames of blue, yellow and orange caressed its feathers as it let out a high-pitched screech which filled the room.

'Stand fast!' shouted India. 'We must stand fast to allow them safe passage.'

The four women clung to each other as they were buffeted by the wind and fire that spun within the sacred circle.

India glanced at the crystal by her feet and watched as its light faltered. 'They're nearly through,' she cried. 'We must hold on.'

The phoenix swivelled its flaming head and rested its glassy black eyes on India.

'Goddess protect me,' she whispered.

The intense heat closed in around them, sucking the oxygen from the room until they were each struggling to breathe. India's eyes were burning, and she turned her face away as they chanted the protection spell over and over.

In a wild flurry of feather and flames, the great bird reared up and spread its wings. A riot of red, orange and black filled the tiny space as the bird screeched. It launched forward, spewing forth fire and ash. Beating its wings, the creature screamed. India could feel the magical connection begin to waver.

'Stand fast,' she shouted once more into the hurricane, urging her coven to hold on, but before the crystal's light was doused completely the phoenix roared again and vanished through the whirling space.

The room was plunged into darkness, and India hurried to turn on the storeroom light, feeling her way over boxes until she found the light switch.

As she switched the light on, a scream filled the air.

The brilliant red of the pentagram had turned black where the symbol had been burnt into the wood. All but one of the shaken witches stood on their point. Lydia lay on the floor a few feet beyond the circle, the line of salt scattered where her feet had broken its protection. Her head was bent at an impossible angle and her lifeless eyes were frozen in a look of terror.

'Amber…Connor…' Hettie looked at India as she wept for her fallen sister.

India nodded. 'They made it through, barely…' Gently she covered Lydia's body with a blanket, '…I just don't know how they're going to get home.'

Swallowing down the overwhelming grief that threatened to erupt from every pore in her body, she faced what was left of her coven.

'We can't reopen the gateway without a fourth coven member. That's the only way they can get home.'

Chapter 9

The wall of flames vanished quickly, and they ran as fast as they could along the scorched tunnel. As they approached the end, the flames began to flicker along the walls.

'It's not going to hold for much longer,' Amber shouted.

They pushed onward, sprinting for the opening of the tunnel and barely clearing the end just as the flames roared once more.

'That was close,' Connor panted, resting one hand on his knee and patting out a rogue flame on his trouser leg, 'I thought they would have given us a bit longer.'

The end of the tunnel opened up into a wide cave which twisted further down into the earth. It was a gaping hole of utter blackness, and as Connor fished out the torch from his rucksack, Amber tried to calm her nerves.

They inched forward slowly, their boots scratching the hard rock, lurching over debris and tree roots that snaked out of the walls.

The light from Connor's torch bounced macabre silhouettes across the roof of the cave. Their breathing was erratic as they descended lower into the belly of the earth.

Amber tripped, instinctively thrusting her hands out to stop herself, but she landed on the compacted soil, her knees impacting hard, and she winced at the sudden shock.

The smell of rotting vegetation mixed with the metallic scent of blood filled her nostrils and she screwed up her face in disgust.

'They've been here,' she hissed into the darkness. 'I can smell the same stench that covered Dan that night in the graveyard.'

Connor took her hand and gave it a squeeze. 'I won't let anything hurt you.'

Despite the inky gloom and oppressive atmosphere, Amber smiled. They hadn't spoken about their impulsive kiss and subsequent lack of communication. In fact the whole event had been swept under the proverbial rug, but she knew Connor would protect her with his life if he had to. She just hoped it wouldn't come to that.

A loud scraping sound echoed around them, reverberating off the rock and vibrating through their bones.

Connor spun around in the direction of the sound, dropping the torch. As it crashed to the floor, it went out, plunging them into total blackness.

Amber let out a low scream and pressed her trembling body against the cave wall. It felt cold beneath her thin shirt. The heat of the gateway tunnel didn't reach these depths, and water trickled down the walls, the stone coated with a foul-smelling fungus.

Her fingers shook as she stretched out her arms and searched the air around her for Connor.

'Where are you?' she hissed.

A deep guttural laugh carried through the caves, ricocheting off the walls and enveloping Amber like a murderer's embrace.

'Connor!' Her voice rose with panic and she flinched as she felt an icy touch on her shoulder.

'It's me,' Connor murmured in her ear. 'I'm here.'

Relief washed over her as she grabbed for his hand and clung on tightly.

'Can you get your torch out of your pack?'

She shimmied out of her rucksack and with unsteady fingers fumbled with the clasp. She pulled out the heavy rubber torch and flicked on the switch.

The vivid light flooded the cave as Connor tensed beside her. She raised her eyes and felt all the air rush from her body.

THE MOUTH of the tunnel ahead of them was blocked by a mountainous creature. Its long arms were as muscular as its legs, but Amber's eyes were drawn to the razor-sharp talons on its fingers where fresh blood dripped and pooled at its feet.

Its black eyes scoured the cave, and Amber realised with a short-lived sense of relief that they were hidden from its view by the torch's illumination.

She didn't dare breathe and with her spare hand she squeezed Connor's arm. Moving slowly, he took the light from her rigid grasp and held her other hand.

'Follow me, when I go, you go,' he said in a low voice.

Connor faced the creature and with a roar he lifted the torch so the beam shone directly into the creature's eyes. It screwed up its face and swatted the air with its long arms, howling like an animal caught in a trap.

'Run, now!'

Dragging her behind him, he set off at a sprint, skirting past the momentarily blinded demon, dodging its flailing arms and heading for the mouth of the tunnel. Its razor claws caught the wall just above Amber's head and a shower of stones fell on her as she ran, one lump of rock hitting her full on the forehead. She could feel the damp, hot blood oozing from the cut and running into her eyes, blurring her vision.

She brushed her face with the back of her hand and concentrated on staying upright and moving as fast as her weary legs would take her.

'Come on,' Connor urged her on, as her lungs protested severely.

Just when she thought she might either throw up or pass out, they burst from the mouth of the cave and into a clearing surrounded by trees.

'Wait, please.' She rested her palms on her knees and bent her head low, the impact she'd received from the falling rock causing her head to spin. Her mouth was dry and her heart was hammering in her chest.

'Here.' Connor handed her a bottle of water and she drained its contents gratefully.

There was a deep roar just behind them. She clutched the empty water bottle and shot off after Connor as he ran deeper into the forest.

THE SKY was a blanket of gold and orange, creating an impressive backdrop to the Black Mountains as they stretched across the horizon. Although the sky was still light as they moved through the dense forest, the chill in the air told Amber that dusk was imminent.

She was surprised at how lush the landscape was. With all the talk of fire and brimstone she had been expecting a land not dissimilar to an artist's impression of hell, but instead of rivers of red and geysers spewing fire bolts she was looking at tall trees with black gnarled bark and green leaves. The floor was a blanket of moss interspersed with tiny blue flowers and to her left, through the rows of tree trunks, she could see a field of wild flowers.

Her stomach growled and she realised neither she nor Connor had eaten anything since the bacon and eggs India had prepared that morning.

She was about to suggest they stop for food when Connor dropped flat to the floor, hissing for her to follow his lead.

Without any question she lay on the moss next to him and peered through the undergrowth at what had spooked him.

On the path ahead of them, partially hidden among trees, was a large cat, its black coat as dark as obsidian. It reminded her of a panther, aside from the sharp tusks protruding from its upper lip and the red spots covering its hide. As they watched, the creature sniffed the air and swung its head in their direction.

She held her breath, for what seemed like the millionth time that day, as the creature growled, causing every hair on her body to stand on end.

It nestled lower to the floor, keeping sharp eyes poised in their direction. If they moved an inch it would be upon them in one leap.

'What are we going to do?' she whispered.

Before Connor could answer, a growl filled the air above them. He cried out for Amber to move, and she rolled her body away just in time to miss the claws of the huge cave creature as it swiped at her. Screaming, she spun into Connor who leapt to his feet pulling her with him.

They were fenced in between the two creatures. Sweat trickled down Amber's forehead, mixing with the dried blood from her cut. She couldn't take her eyes off the advancing creature; its sharp teeth, coated in dark red stains, glistened in the fading light. As it prepared to strike, a flash of black filled the air. The cat pounced, bypassing Amber and Connor and going straight for the lumbering creature, tearing at its throat with its sharp tusks.

Grabbing her hand, Connor ran as fast as he could in the opposite direction. Amber didn't care how much her limbs ached and screamed in resistance, she was relieved to be in one piece and not smeared over the forest floor.

They didn't stop moving for what seemed like hours. She didn't remember when night had taken over, but two bright moons hung heavy in the star-studded sky. She was cold and pulled Tom's hoodie tightly across her chest, taking in his lingering scent. Connor hadn't said two words to her since they escaped the creatures, and the silence between them was stifling. If they were going to be successful with their mission then she would have to speak to him and tell him how she felt.

She wasn't a silly schoolgirl with a penchant for kissing the first boy who drew her a sacred circle. She cared for Connor, more than she probably should, and he needed to know.

'We should be safe to camp here for tonight.'

He had come to a halt in a small clearing and tossed his pack on the floor, looking at her for some sort of response.

'Yeah, this looks good,' she mumbled. 'Can we build a fire?'

'Good idea, I'll collect some wood if you can gather some rocks for the pit circle.'

He began grabbing some of the fallen branches and she took this as her cue to busy herself collecting rocks.

She left her own pack and began scouring the ground for decent-sized stones. Her mind wandered once again to the kiss they had shared. It had been tender and sweet, not a stupid mistake, no matter what Connor had said. He had instigated it, after all.

She shook her head to try to dislodge the memory, and as she stooped down to collect a couple of rocks she heard a sound behind her.

'Connor…is that you?'

No answer.

Her heart raced and her sweaty palms clung to the rocks as she brandished them like weapons.

She gradually backed up until she could feel the rough bark of a tree behind her. Looking around she realised she had no idea which direction she had walked in. She kicked herself for being so wrapped up in her thoughts.

A noise to her right caused her heart to freeze; she could hear heavy breathing, a laboured rhythm. She slowly pulled the hood of her jumper up over her hair and using the shadows of the tree she camouflaged herself against the black bark. Her fingernails dug into the rocks as she listened.

The bushes to her right parted and a Guardian burst through into the clearing, his swords drawn and his red eyes piercing the night, his swirling tattoo clearly displayed as the light of the moon shone down on him. Amber tilted her head down so her hood covered her face and pressed her body against the tree, willing it to open up and swallow her.

The Guardian grunted and moved on, his heavy boots trampling the delicate flowers on the forest floor. He elbowed his way through the bushes, moving in the direction of the Black Mountains.

Amber didn't know whether to laugh or cry, but as she relaxed there was a flash of silver and she felt the pinch of cold steel at her throat.

'What do we have here?' a silky voice breathed into her ear, as a hooded figure pressed the blade harder into her skin. Amber gasped and as her captor tilted her head backwards, her hood fell back and her long hair tumbled around her shoulders, her silver stripe shining in the moonlight.

The figure pulled back then released the blade.

'Myanna?' a male voice asked.

Amber was startled. 'That's my mother's name!'

She pushed herself away from the tree and spoke again with more urgency. 'Please…Myanna is my mother, how do you know her?'

The figure sheathed its blade. He wasn't a Guardian as the build was wrong. This person was lithe as well as muscular but not in the creepy way of the Guardians. With delicate hands he lowered his hood to reveal the most beautiful face Amber had ever seen. She inhaled sharply as the boy's long white hair spilled down his back and his purple eyes searched her face.

'You're a faerie,' she said.

The boy cocked his head to the side, taking her in, 'I am a fae warrior from Queen Alia's court, what are you?'

Amber smiled. 'I thought I was a sixteen-year-old girl until a few days ago but apparently I'm…not.'

She stopped herself from revealing her oracle heritage. She didn't know this boy and she was well aware of the powers of persuasion the fae possessed. She needed to learn more about him before she poured her heart out to him, even though that's exactly what she wanted to do.

'How do you know my mother?'

'She is a member of the fae queen's court, a trusted friend of Queen Alia.'

'Queen Alia? I don't understand. I thought Phelan was a Guardian realm, not Fae.'

'Queen Alia is fae, she was taken captive by General Loso many years ago. She is kept here as a prisoner at the top of the Black Mountains in the Guardian stronghold.'

'Wait, so you're saying my mother…Myanna…is here, in Phelan?'

'Yes, she is with the queen, a prisoner too.'

Amber slumped back against the tree and rubbed her face.

'You're hurt.' The boy lifted his hand and stroked Amber's forehead. Tiny bursts of electricity shot along her skin at his touch, and she had the strongest sensation of familiarity.

He studied the deep cut on her forehead, his face just inches from hers, then pulled a cloth from his pocket.

'Come.' Lightly he took her hand and pulled her along behind him, a strange pulse vibrating through her body at his touch. After a few minutes of walking, Amber could hear the sound of rushing water, and as they stepped out of the darkness of the forest she saw a beautiful clearing with a deep lagoon and waterfall illuminated in the moonlight.

He left her side to rinse the cloth in the water, and when he returned he carefully pressed the cool fabric to her head. Amber reached up and held her own hand over the boy's.

'What's your name?'

'Redka of Avaveil.'

'Redka.' She listened to the sound of his name on her tongue, 'I like that. I'm Amber.'

Their faces were close again and Amber could smell the sweet scent of jasmine mixed with the woody tang of the forest. Redka's purple eyes glistened in the moonlight. Amber felt like she was falling into a whirlpool and would disappear any second. She knew this boy, had seen him somewhere before. They were connected, she could feel it deep within her soul, but she couldn't remember how.

The sound of a snapping branch broke through her thoughts as Redka pulled her gently into the darkness of a nearby tree. He lifted her hood over her hair again and shielded her body with his own, pressing close to her and enveloping them in the dark shadows of the forest, his black cape disguising the brightness of his own hair as he stretched the fabric to cloak them.

'There are many Guardians in the forest, we don't want them stumbling upon us, it would be bad for both of us if we were discovered.'

As he pressed his body against her and she inhaled his scent, she was convinced he would feel her heart beating out of her ribcage. A strange vibration pulsed through her veins and she shivered, all practical thoughts floating out of her head. The feeling that this boy was linked to her in some way was too strong to shake off. She had never believed in love at first sight, but as she rested her forehead against the curve of his shoulder, she couldn't help but wonder if this is what it would feel like.

A figure broke through the bushes, carrying a torch. Amber rested her hand on Redka's chest. 'It's okay, it's Connor, and he's my friend.'

He moved to let her pass, and she ran to Connor as he blindly searched the water and surrounding shrubbery.

'Connor, I'm here.'

'Bloody hell, Amber, I thought they'd taken you. I saw a Guardian and then I couldn't find you, I was so…' His voice trailed off as Redka walked up behind her.

His eyes didn't give anything away as he looked from Amber to the newcomer.

'I was tending to Amber's wounds.' Redka's voice was hypnotic as he explained his presence.

Connor nodded stiffly and Amber noticed his eyes shift to purple.

'I am Redka, warrior to Queen Alia's court.' He held his hand across his chest and bowed slightly.

Connor coughed dryly. 'I'm Connor, warrior for Amber's court.'

Amber rolled her eyes and excused herself from the testosterone-charged exchange, convinced that any minute they would be comparing scars.

She walked to the water's edge and rinsed the cloth in her hand. The lagoon was beautiful, surrounded by green trees on three sides and flanked by a wall of rock where the water cascaded over the top to fall in a foaming mass in the centre of the pool.

Beyond the treeline she could just see the top of the Black Mountains. Her mum was there and her best friend. Her head reeled at the thought of her mother. She wondered if they were together, if Tom would recognise her and ask for help.

She was overcome with a sudden tiredness, the strain of the day catching up with her, and she settled herself on the ground to listen to the gentle lull of the waterfall. Redka and Connor's hushed voices played around in the deep recesses of her mind, their words fading as her eyes fluttered shut.

She was running through the forest with Redka and Connor by her side. There were others with her and she frantically searched for a familiar face in the crowd. Redka had drawn his sword and faced a Guardian. There was a bloody fight and the Guardian fell. They ran further and further into the forest, the lush green crumbling around them to reveal black rock. Another Guardian stepped forward, this one much larger, his eyes glowing a deeper red. His armour was different from the other soldiers'; the phoenix crest was golden. Redka drew his sword, blocking the man's path, but then he fell, pitching to his knees. Amber could see the dagger buried in his chest and his lifeless purple eyes stared at her as she screamed.

CHAPTER 10

The sound of rushing water tore Amber from her dreams. They were so realistic now that she was often disoriented upon waking, as if she had witnessed these events for real. She always awoke with the heavy weight of loss in her heart.

Lavanya had told her she had the sight, the gift of prophecy, but she didn't want it if she had to watch her friends suffer over and over.

'Morning.' Connor was adding wood to the fire. He looked up and smiled, his face shining in the brightness of the new day. He looked at home here in the forest, more than he had in Hills Heath.

'What time is it?'

'Still early, the sun doesn't stay down for long in Phelan.'

She looked around the small makeshift campsite, her eyes searching every square inch.

'He's gone to find some breakfast.' Connor's voice was low as Amber blushed and kicked at a stone in the dirt.

'I wasn't...' she started to say but Connor cut her off.

'Don't lie, you have a connection, any idiot can see that. His eyes were glowing purple and your aura was blazing bright gold...not so good when you're trying to hide from demons, by the way.'

Amber felt her face grow hotter and she lifted her hands to cover her cheeks. A golden aura. She didn't even realise Connor could see auras, and she wasn't sure she wanted him seeing hers when she didn't know what it was doing.

'It's a fae thing,' he said as if understanding her silent question. 'I can see what people are feeling by the colours they give off. It was really weak back home but this place has amplified my fae powers. Right now your aura is red, which means you are either really horny or pissed at me.'

'Connor!' She couldn't help but laugh at him. He gave her a cheeky smile and her heart turned over in her chest. A brief memory of their shared kiss sprang to mind, but she hastily buried it in her subconscious. The oddest feeling of guilt washed over her for even thinking of it.

She watched Connor as he stoked the fire, his tousled brown hair curled at the nape of his neck and his fringe flopped across his face. As he blew on the embers, she noticed how defined his strong cheekbones were. The recollection of their kiss bubbled to the surface again, and she memorised how she had clung to him as he ran his hands along the curve of her spine. She shivered involuntarily.

'Are you cold?' He stood and draped a blanket across her shoulders, then took a seat next to her on the moss-covered floor and gazed into the fire. His nearness and the smell of his clothes were intoxicating. What was wrong with her? She shook her head trying to dislodge the image of their entwined bodies.

'What's the plan then?' She needed a distraction and strategising helped.

'Redka said it's not too far to the foot of the Black Mountains. He can get us into the stronghold through tunnels in the rock. Apparently no-one knows they exist, which works in our favour.'

'My mum is here,' she said softly, staring at the shapes dancing in the flames.

'Yeah, after you fell asleep, Redka filled me in on the list of prisoners. Looks like Tom is in good company.'

'What if he didn't make it? Lavanya said he was weak but still alive, that was a few days ago, what if he couldn't hold on?' Tears tumbled from her eyes; she didn't try to hide them, instead she gratefully accepted the hug Connor offered. He wrapped his arms around her and squeezed gently.

'He's a tough lad and he knows in his heart that you will find a way to save him, you've never let each other down before.'

She nodded at this; it was true. They had been an inseparable team for so long that they could finish each other's sentences and feel what the other was going through. School bullies, overly aggressive superiors, stepmothers – Tom had been with her through it all and she with him.

'About the other night, in the magic shop…' She stood to warm herself by the fire, hoping to gain some strength from the warmth it gave out. Connor shifted position on the floor and opened his mouth to say something just as Redka emerged from the trees. She felt her body quiver at the sight of him, and as he gazed at her she saw the anguish in his eyes on seeing her upset.

'What's wrong?' he asked, taking her hand in his own. He used his free hand to wipe away the last of her tears, his purple eyes boring deep into her soul. She melted against him as he swept her up in an embrace.

'Just a little overwhelmed,' she said smiling up into his beautiful face, 'I'm about to see my mum again after ten years, my dad is missing and I'm worried about my friend.'

He nodded and held her by the shoulders. 'Your friend is strong. He was badly injured, but your mother is a skilled witch and is tending to his wounds. Please don't fear for them.'

Amber stepped away from him. 'My mother is…' She struggled to find the right words. 'Is she injured at all or ill?'

Redka shook his head and motioned for her to sit. 'When Queen Alia was kidnapped, she was dragged through many realms before arriving in Phelan. There is no gateway between this world and the land of the fae, so the journey was long. General Loso didn't realise she was with child when he took her, and so by the time they arrived here she was heavily pregnant.' He paused to add a log to the fire, staring at the flames for a moment. Amber waited patiently for him to continue as Connor settled beside her to listen.

'She had her baby and Loso built her a fortress which was also her prison. She raised her son and kept him safe, but the reason for her capture soon became evident. Loso began taking her blood and injecting it into his own body using similar blood magic to the Guardian ritual. He believed this would make him immortal.'

Amber gasped. 'Is that true?'

'Yes, the fae live for a long time, fifty years pass for every human year in our realm, but we can still be killed. A royal's blood is much more potent and contains the magic of healing and immortality. Loso feared that his own captains were going to turn on him, and so he used Queen Alia's blood to make him invincible.'

'Did it work?' Connor asked.

'It did. One of his captains in the south ran him through with a sword but Loso just pulled the sword from his heart and laughed then beheaded the surprised captain. Word spread and the entire realm now believes Loso to be immortal.'

'What happened to the queen?'

'She became very ill, having her blood drained so often meant that her body couldn't heal in time before Loso took more. It became a drug to him.' Redka sighed deeply and his shoulders sagged. 'She nearly died and that's almost impossible for a royal fae.'

'I take it she's still alive then?'

'That's where your mother comes in,' he said, turning to Amber and smiling. 'When the queen was at her worst, Loso realised that his actions may just kill her, and he admitted to me that he cared deeply for her, so he ordered two of his best soldiers to accompany him to the human realm and kidnap a witch with healing powers.'

'My mother vanished ten years ago.' Amber felt sick; she and her dad had believed that Myanna had left them because she didn't care, started a new life somewhere else without them.

'Yes, I remember when the witch arrived to heal the queen, she was strong-willed and feisty. She even tried to break the pact Loso had built with the human witches back in your realm. She is the most amazing healer I have ever seen.'

Something stirred inside Amber – pride.

'So my mother was taken from us and brought to Phelan to nurse a dying queen of the fae? Is the queen still sick?'

'No, she is fully restored to health.'

'So why didn't the general let my mother go?' Her eyes began to sting and her voice rose slightly as she questioned the reason her mother hadn't seen her grow up.

'Queen Alia and your mother are incredibly close. I don't think she would leave her side even if Loso ordered it. I told you, she is strong-willed.'

Connor rubbed his hand across his face and addressed Redka, 'What happened to the baby that Queen Alia had?'

Amber snapped her head up to look at Redka as he stood and swung round to face them.

He bent over in a deep bow, folding his arm across his chest as he spoke, 'Prince Redka of Avaveil at your service.'

Amber's mouth hung wide open as she watched this beautiful boy give a sheepish shrug of his muscular shoulders. Connor snorted with laughter.

'Great...a prince, that figures.'

Amber squeezed the bridge of her nose between her fingers and tried to take it all in. Queen Alia was a prisoner and had given birth to Redka here in Phelan. When she got sick, her own mother had been kidnapped to save her and was also a prisoner. Her best friend had been kidnapped and he too was a prisoner. She was looking forward to meeting this General Loso; she had a lot she wanted to say to him.

THE JOURNEY through Phelan, up to the Black Mountains was a quiet one; all three were lost in their own thoughts and only stopped briefly to refill their water bottles at another lagoon. Amber marvelled again at the beauty of such a violent realm. The trees stood tall and proud, and the meadows and bubbling brooks looked like something Monet had painted. The colours were vivid; a sea of pink, purple, blue and yellow splashed across the landscape.

The Black Mountains didn't look as sinister as she had imagined, and as she followed Redka through the forests and open pastures, she longed to stay, to lie amongst the flowers and peer up at the blue sky, to rest in the shadow of the mountain with her prince.

Her prince – she shook her head to clear her mind. Redka wasn't *her* prince, yes he was a prince but he wasn't her prince, was he? As she watched his square shoulders, from her position behind him on the track, she allowed herself a moment to dream. The muscles on his arms were evident through his dark shirt, and his long white hair was tied in a braid down his back, bound by leather cord. Caught in the warm breeze, wisps were flying about his shoulders and face as he walked. As if sensing her staring, he swung around.

'Is everything okay?'

She walked faster, catching up to stride alongside him. 'Yes, fine, I was just thinking what a beautiful place Phelan is.'

He laughed, a loud deep laugh which lit up his face.

'That's Queen Alia's doing.' He swept his arm in a wide arc and spun around in a full circle. 'From the fortress, the queen can see all of these lands. She didn't like what she saw when she arrived, so she used her elemental magic and altered the scenery.'

Amber was stunned. 'She can do that?'

'Yes, most fae have elemental magic, even Connor here.'

Connor caught up with them.

'Can you?' Amber asked him. 'Can you change nature?'

He shrugged and picked up a bright blue flower from the ground; he held it closely in the palm of his hand and closed his eyes. As they watched, the flower turned yellow.

'Ha, I guess I can!'

'That's amazing.' She took the flower from Connor and examined it incredulously.

'So what was the scenery like before your mum used her faerie mojo on it?' Connor asked as they set off walking again.

'Ah, when we reach the mountains I will be able to show you. Alia's fortress faces east with no windows to the north, south or west, so the rest of Phelan looks as it always looked, pretty nasty.'

Amber still held the yellow flower in her hand as she trailed behind the boys; she recalled her conversation with Lavanya when she had been in her dream state. She had been told that her powers were strong and that she possessed all seven of the ancient oracle powers. She remembered that elemental magic was one of them.

She concentrated on her third eye until she could feel her hands tingling and then dug down deep to find her sacral chakra. The colour orange flooded her vision, and as she directed the power into the tiny yellow flower, it burst into flames, curling and turning to ash in her open palm.

She jumped and dropped the remains.

'You okay?' Connor called back to her from further along the path.

'Yes…I'm fine, thought I saw a bug.' She wasn't ready to tell them about her gifts yet, and she didn't want to tell Connor she had just destroyed something so brutally, after he had used his fae gifts on it; he had been so pleased with himself. She was going to have to be careful with her powers and learn to use them in secret before unleashing them on her unsuspecting friends.

Shaking off the shock of her newfound skill with fire, she watched Redka and Connor walking ahead of her and marvelled at how two boys could be so perfect. They had different colourings, Connor with his dark brown hair and mocha eyes, and Redka with strong fae genes of pure white hair and piercing purple eyes. He was also a touch taller, but they were both muscular, tall and beautiful. She felt her heart lurch first one way and then the other, like a warped game of spin the bottle, but the bottle never stopped in one place. She was now tied to both of them and had the strangest feeling that the bonds ran deeper than any of them could imagine.

Chapter II

Redka hadn't been joking about the state of Phelan. As they climbed the lower half of the Black Mountains, Amber could see the lands that Queen Alia's elemental magic hadn't reached.

The ground was scorched; the sky was heavy with clouds of ash from the hundreds of open craters where the lava had been forced through the earth's crust. There were no trees, no fields of flowers, only fire, rivers of lava and demons.

Amber had been ready to run when they spotted the mountainous creatures. Her initial interaction in the cave had been unpleasant, swiftly followed by a near decapitation in the forest. She was happy to stay as far away from the Dragovax as possible.

'Do not fear, they are only hunting for the lavahogs that live in the rock crevices. Phelan is their homeland,' Redka explained as they climbed the rock face. 'The Guardians invaded this realm thousands of years ago when their own homeland was overtaken by dragons.'

Amber was about to exclaim that nobody had told her dragons were real when they reached a small opening in the rock. Redka grasped her hand and pulled her up onto the rocky outcropping. Tiny bursts of heat coursed through her body as their palms connected. He didn't seem to notice, or chose to remain silent, as he moved to help Connor.

The opening was a small hole in the rock face, like an empty eye socket chiselled out of stone. They had to crouch to fit through the gap; Redka led the way, his faerie sight allowing him to see clearly in the gloom.

Once they had shuffled through the opening, the tunnel roof sloped higher, making it a little easier to navigate. As she walked deeper into the mountain, Amber could feel her hands and feet begin to tingle. She concentrated her energies on her third eye and felt a cool rush of air envelop her body.

She heard Connor exhale behind her. 'Holy cow!'

Redka stopped walking and looked back at them.

'Amber…you're glowing like a firefly.' His voice was hushed as he took in the sight of Amber wrapped in the subtle yellow glow of the tiny flames that licked her aura. They didn't burn, instead they flickered and caressed her clothing and hair, projecting a buttery light and casting soft shadows on the tunnel walls.

'Great, we have our own human torch,' Connor teased. 'Lead the way.'

'I get the distinct impression that Amber is not human,' Redka added.

'No shit, Sherlock,' Connor mumbled before pressing his hand on the small of Amber's back and gently pushing her forward.

'I'm an oracle,' Amber said very matter-of-factly as she walked along the now well-lit stone corridor.

Redka's eyes widened and he opened his mouth as if about to speak then closed it again. Amber felt the warm glow in her stomach at being able to shock him into a stunned silence, proud of her newly-discovered destiny for the first time. She pushed gently past him and trailed her hand along the black rock, feeling the bumps and grooves with her fingertips. As she rounded a bend, the corridor spilled out into a small circular cave, the walls rough and cold to the touch. A rickety ladder had been leant against the cavern wall and went up as far as Amber could see; even her muted oracle illumination couldn't reach the top.

'It's a long climb,' Redka said, as if reading her mind. 'When we reach the surface, we will be in a small food store within the fortress. It's where the animal feed is kept, but not many of the Guardians stay there for long as the smell is quite rancid.' He wrinkled his nose up to emphasise how bad it was. 'The animals shouldn't bother us if we move slowly and stay close to the walls.'

'What animals do they keep?' Amber couldn't imagine a race of evil warriors keeping goats or puppies.

'Razor warriors,' he replied, placing his feet on the bottom rung of the ladder. 'They are vicious cats with tusks as sharp as knives. If you were a demon they would rip you apart, but they seem to like everyone else.'

'Think we already met one, a big black cat saved us from a demon attack just as we cleared the gateway, I'm guessing that's your razor warrior.'

'Sounds like it; once they smell the blood of the demons they go a little crazy.'

They began to climb, slowly at first, but once they got into a rhythm then the climbing became easier and quicker. Before she knew it Redka was offering her his hand and pulling her up into a large hole in the ground above, with a wooden trapdoor. There was a rancid odour, like decaying carcases intermingled with the sweet, sickly smell of rotting fruit.

Redka lifted the trapdoor. The insipid light of the storeroom was just enough to allow him to check for soldiers. Amber doused her internal flashlight.

Outside the door she could discern mounds of cloth dotted across the floor. Redka inched the door open just enough for them all to slip through, then closed it and slid the bolt home.

They blended into the shadows with their backs against the stone wall of the pens. Amber noticed, with a rising feeling of nausea, that the mounds of cloth were in fact bits of demons. There was an arm here, a leg there and an eyeball or three nestled among the flagstones. She covered her mouth and looked at her feet, fearful that if she looked again she would throw up over everyone.

Connor silently slipped his hand into hers and squeezed. She looked at him and he gave her a gentle smile; her aura must have been a puce green or something for him to notice she wasn't coping very well.

Redka circled the pen, keeping to the shadows; two Guardians marched past causing him to freeze on the spot. Their red eyes gleamed in the dim light as they checked on the animals. The razor warriors didn't seem to notice or care about the intrusion and busied themselves ripping into the demon meat that littered the floor.

Amber didn't think she could hold on to the contents of her stomach much longer and nudged Redka in the back to urge him on. He gave a small nod and slipped open the cage door to let them all out.

'How come you have to hide from the Guardians if you've lived here all your life?' Connor hissed as they spewed out into the dank corridor.

Redka chuckled. 'As far as Loso and the soldiers are aware I have never left the fortress. I train in the arena and I live in the queen's staterooms, and they seem pleased with that. I, on the other hand, ventured outside as soon as I could walk, finding or making secret passages.' He looked pointedly at Amber, 'I knew the day would come when we would flee, and I needed to be ready to guide my family out of here.'

Amber hurried to the small window opposite the pen and gulped in a lungful of air to steady her stomach, then began choking as the soot hit the back of her throat. The window looked out across the mountain range; huge black rocks jutted out from the earth tinged red from the flames that burst through the craters. A river of red lava wound its way through the landscape until it met with a sea of burning orange at the foot of the mountain. The horizon was bright red, like the sky was bleeding.

'Why on earth would anyone *want* to invade this realm and set up home?'

Redka looked over Amber's shoulder. 'Can you understand why Queen Alia altered the view?'

Connor took a look at Phelan and shuddered. 'I'm just glad the gateway we came through was in the east!'

They made their way through the fortress like thieves pulling off a dangerous heist, slinking into the shadows at the sound of footsteps and motioning silent instructions to each other as they headed deeper into the building.

The place was vast, and Amber noticed, as Redka had already pointed out, that the windows only faced east. The view was much better this way, and the air was filled with a much more pleasant scent of blossom and grass.

'Is this what Avaveil looks like?' she asked Redka as they slipped past a bank of windows.

A shadow descended over his face. 'I believe so. Unfortunately I was born in Phelan, so I've never seen the land of the fae for myself, and only through Queen Alia's eyes can I see the true beauty of my home realm.'

'If we succeed then you may get to see your true homeland for real.' Amber's heart faltered at the thought that she may have to leave him in the future. Her mission was to save Tom – and now her mother – and return to Hills Heath in the human realm; he belonged in Avaveil with his mother and his people.

Redka strode ahead to catch up with Connor, as Amber's chest grew tight from a loss that hadn't happened yet. She felt a tear slide slowly down her cheek. Reaching up she caught it in her hand; a single tear full of love and fear. As she watched, the tear crystallised to form a perfect tiny diamond. She closed her palm around the stone, her thoughts shifting briefly to Lavanya and her own oracle heritage.

THE BOYS had moved far ahead of her and were nearly at the end of the long walkway; the corridor was made up of a long stone wall with a single wooden door to her right and windows to her left. As she hurried to catch up with them, the door opened in front of her, cutting off her escape. She glanced wildly around her but there was nowhere to hide. She stood her ground as a figure walked out of the annexe room and closed the door behind them. She willed the boys to turn around and see her predicament.

The figure wore a long blue cloak with a cowl edged with gold embroidery; a basket of herbs swung from the person's arm and they were humming a hypnotic tune. Amber relaxed slightly as she realised this wasn't a Guardian but one of the household staff.

As Connor and Redka spun around to look down the corridor, the figure faltered and stopped humming.

'Redka?' It was a soft female voice. 'What are you doing here? Who are you with?'

As if sensing a presence behind her, the cloaked woman slowly pivoted, and her hood fell back to reveal long brown curls with a silver strand of hair framing a beautiful face.

'Mum?' A sob wracked through Amber at the sight of her mother.

'Amber!' She dropped the basket and ran towards her, sweeping her into her arms as they wept in unison.

They clung to one another as the boys herded them back into the annexe room so they wouldn't be discovered.

The room was simple; an old timber table sat in the centre and the walls were lined with shelves of herbs, spices and ointments. The smells were intoxicating.

Myanna clung to her daughter. 'What are you doing here? How did you find this place?' Her face was red with crying and her voice wavered as she spoke.

'Tom was taken by a Guardian, and I came with Connor…' She jerked her thumb at Connor who nodded his head by way of a polite introduction. 'We came through the gateway to save Tom and then we met Redka and he told me you were here and I…we thought you left us.' Another wave of tears washed over her, and she buried her face in her mother's long hair, breathing in her long-forgotten scent.

Myanna soothed her daughter, stroking her back and winding her long hair around her small fist. 'It's far too dangerous for you here. If Loso finds you I can't imagine what he would do to you.'

'I know, Mum, but I couldn't leave Tom to the fate of the Guardians.' She sighed deeply, feeling the full weight of the responsibility she had placed upon herself. 'I know that I'm an oracle. Connor and

Lavanya have been teaching me to connect with my powers. It may help to free him.'

Her mother gasped. 'You didn't show any signs of having powers when you were smaller. We thought we had made a mistake and the prophecies were mistaken.'

'Oh, they're real. I guess my powers would have emerged eventually but I was cursed by Dad's girlfriend.'

'Excuse me!' Myanna placed her hands squarely on her tiny hips.

Amber suddenly felt like a six-year-old again and, realising her error, she stammered, 'Oh no, it's not what you think, he was cursed too, we both were.'

'By a necromancer,' Connor interjected.

'We must get you to the queen.'

Myanna hunted through an old wicker basket and dug out two navy cloaks, each one lavishly decorated with tiny stars made from silver thread. She handed them to Amber and Connor who put them on, and then she led them back out into the corridor. They hurried along the dusty flagstones keeping their heads low.

The long walkway eventually opened up into a great hall, rectangular in shape. Stone pillars ran through the centre like silent guards. The entire floor was made up of a mosaic of intricate patterns with a huge red phoenix at the centre. On the far wall there was a raised platform made from black rock, likely mined from the Black Mountains. A single stone throne sat in the centre, and to the left a row of marble tables flanked the wall, each one tainted deep red.

Amber looked away; she knew the stains were blood.

As if he realised her thoughts, Redka placed his hand on her shoulder. 'They are used in the Guardian ritual,' he whispered. 'Human blood is drained out of the body and Guardian blood put back in.'

'How do the boys stay alive through the ritual?'

'Magic. Loso uses my mother to hold the souls in limbo until the Guardian blood is in place.'

Amber's eyes grew wide. 'She can do that?'

'It is a complicated spell, one normally reserved for the fae; when one of my kind die it is the queen's job to ensure their soul reaches the Plains of Avaveil, a sacred place where we can be reincarnated as a part of nature. Loso forces my mother to do the ritual on the boys so they can survive the bloodletting.'

'How can he force her to do such a thing?' Amber had the oddest feeling she didn't want to hear the answer.

Redka paused for a long moment before answering. 'If my mother doesn't do as he asks, then Loso will kill me…and Myanna.'

Chapter 12

Queen Alia was beautiful. More beautiful than anyone Amber had ever seen. Her long white hair hung in spirals around her delicate shoulders, bouncing as she floated across the floor to greet them. Her delicate frame was swathed in a huge white gown studded with tiny diamonds, each one twinkling under the candlelight; the bodice was sculpted to her tiny waist and had capped sleeves of white lace.

Her arms were encased in silver bracelets, and as she moved they tinkled together creating a melody to match her effortless grace. Although her beauty took Amber's breath away, it was the enormous iridescent wings that rose up behind her and fluttered slightly that surprised Amber.

'Welcome, little eye.'

Huge purple eyes framed by thick lashes gazed at Amber, and she felt a slight pull on her mind as if someone had just plugged her into a power socket and flipped the switch.

'Thank you Queen Alia...Your Majesty.' She curtseyed and bowed her head to the floor.

Redka laughed behind her, and Amber shot him a disapproving look.

Alia walked to her son and wagged her finger under his nose. 'At least *she* has good manners, my son.'

It was Amber's turn to laugh now. She liked Queen Alia.

The queen invited the small party to be seated. As they moved out to the garden room, Amber grabbed Redka's sleeve. 'Where are your wings?'

Redka looked at her with a wide smile. Only female fae have wings.'

THE ROOM was almost as beautifully decorated as Alia; the stone walls were hidden by four huge tapestries depicting the changing seasons, vases of fresh flowers and bowls of fruit were dotted on low tables and the seating area comprised of colourful cushions scattered across the floor circling a single wingback chair. The garden room took its name from the wall of windows overlooking the impressive gardens which ended in a high stone wall and shielded the forest beyond.

The doors had been opened and the sweet scent of jasmine wafted in. Amber was suddenly aware of how dirty and unkempt she must look.

'Please excuse our appearance, Your Majesty,' she said, holding her hands out wide. 'We had a tough trip to get here.'

Queen Alia chuckled. 'Please call me Alia, there are no formalities in prison.'

Amber had forgotten that this stunning fortress home was also Alia's prison and had been for many years.

She sat next to her mother and snuggled up beside her just as she had as a small child. She smelt of cinnamon and Amber inhaled the scent, never wanting to forget this moment. Her mind wandered guiltily to her father, and she wondered if India had managed to locate him yet. It was going to be her finest moment when she reunited her parents and vanquished Patricia from their lives.

'You travelled through the gateway of flames.' It was a statement rather than a question. 'May I ask how you managed to drop the wall of fire?'

Connor cleared his throat. 'My aunt is a witch. Her coven were able to duplicate Father Ashby's original spell from when the pact was made between our realm and Phelan. They were able to drop the wall for us but not for long, we only just made it through.' He lifted his charred piece of trouser leg and gave her a crooked smile.

'Your aunt is very powerful, that is not an easy spell to attempt. The gateway is guarded by the phoenix.'

'We didn't see any phoenix, ma'am, but we did bump into a few natives.'

Alia smiled warmly at him. 'Ah yes, the Dragovax, I haven't had the pleasure myself.'

'Do you know why we're here?' Amber interjected, desperate for some news on Tom.

Alia studied her for a while then moved her gaze along to Myanna, 'You are here for a boy, a prisoner.'

'Yes – Tom, he's my friend.'

Her mother spoke quietly. 'He's alive, sweetheart. He looks pretty bad but he's hanging in there.'

'Did you recognise him?'

'Yes, I saw the Guardians herding the boys through the hall, and although he's a lot taller than the last time I saw him, I did recognise his face.' She smiled as she recalled the last time she had seen them together. 'I think the two of you had just built a den in the back garden using my best sheets and a garden stake.'

Amber laughed. 'And it collapsed the minute we got inside.' Her heart ached. Thinking back to good times they had shared was what kept her going, but it was draining her energy to stay so strong. 'Please will you help us to rescue him, to rescue all of them?'

Alia looked at each of the group in turn with a steady gaze. 'I believe we may be able to assist each other.'

Amber wanted to throw her arms around her and hug her tightly, but remembering that she was royalty – and the huge wings – she settled for a cheesy grin instead.

'Where do we start?'

'There will be a ceremony,' Alia told them. 'I will be called upon to perform a spell to make sure the boys survive the bloodletting.

Once this is complete, the prisoners will be taken to the great hall one at a time for the main ceremony. I have already been called to perform once...'

'That was for Dan,' Amber mumbled. 'He's a Guardian now.'

Alia bowed her head, 'I understand that this is hard, but I do everything in my power to help these boys feel as little pain as possible.'

Amber flinched.

Redka cut in, 'If we want to rescue them, then we need to do it before the spell is cast.'

'I agree,' Alia nodded. 'They are kept on the west side of the fortress, the prisoner cells are cut out of volcanic rock with no windows. Their sight will be impaired for a while until they can adjust to the light.'

'The only time they are brought out of the cells is for the shaving,' Redka added.

Amber and Connor shook their heads. 'The what?'

'The prisoners have their heads shaved. You may have noticed the Guardians all look alike: no hair, red eyes, muscular physique. Loso strips away all their human qualities, including hair.'

Redka stroked his own long braid. 'He's never getting his hands on mine.'

Amber pictured Tom; his blond spiky hair was his pride and joy. He was always fiddling with gel and a comb until he got it just right.

'So, the rescue has to take place ahead of the spell and preferably before the shaving?' Connor asked the group.

'It's the best time,' Redka confirmed. 'They use one Guardian to transport them to the southern courtyard for the shaving. They are too disoriented from being kept in the dark, so that is the best time to strike.'

'When's this going to happen?' Amber asked, her jaw set in a hard line. She didn't want to waste another minute. She wanted to get the job done and get home. Her dad needed her too, and she was trying hard to push those thoughts to the back of her mind so she could concentrate on the task at hand, but his image kept pushing its way into her thoughts.

'The next ceremony is set for tomorrow night. You will rest in my court and dress as my servants so you don't draw attention to yourselves. The shaving will take place after dark, so we will have to move just before dusk.' Alia clapped her hands and a short tubby woman with pink wings shuffled into the room.

'Maggie, we need food and water for our guests and fresh clothing. The time has come to prepare for our return to Avaveil.'

Maggie's plump face broke into a wide grin and she bustled off to attend to her chores.

Alia addressed the small group. 'We will do everything we can to rescue your friend, but we can only take you back to your gateway before we must part ways. Our home is Avaveil and we cannot travel with you to your human realm.' Her eyes rested briefly on Myanna, and Amber felt her mother tense next to her. 'You will need the gateway key to enter the human realm. Loso carries this on a chain around his neck. I can get this for you, but if I fail, do you have another way to drop the wall of flames?'

Connor nodded. 'Yes ma'am, my aunt and her coven are ready for our return.'

She smiled at him then turned to her son. 'Is everything in place for our return?'

'Yes, but it hasn't been tested.'

'No matter, your skills are unique and I trust your judgement.' She placed a hand on his arm and smiled before excusing herself from the room.

Amber wrinkled her brow, confused; once Alia had left she questioned her mother.

'What did she mean part ways? I thought there was no gateway between Phelan and Avaveil?'

Myanna shook her head. 'There isn't but Redka has been secretly building a faerie ring deep in the forest for many years with the hope that one day we could escape.'

Amber was stunned. '*We* could escape? – you're not going with them, are you? Not now?'

Myanna squirmed as she answered. 'It's complicated.'

Amber couldn't believe what she was hearing. 'But you belong with me and Dad, back in Hills Heath, not in some faerie realm.' She was aware that her voice had risen and both Connor and Redka had stopped talking to listen to their conversation.

'Of course I want to be with you and Alan, but it's been ten years, Amber, I have to think it through. We have planned for this, planned our escape to Avaveil and then you…you showed up and changed everything.' She hung her head as tears tumbled down her cheeks.

Amber stood up on shaky legs, trying her hardest not to cry. She was used to rejection by now, her dad was a master at pushing her away, but she never thought her own mother would reject her too.

'You're my mum, you belong with your family.'

Myanna looked up into her daughter's face. 'Alia is my family too.'

Amber swivelled on her heel and ran.

Connor found her sulking under an apple tree at the far end of the garden; she was sitting with her back against the rough bark cradling her knees to her chest.

'How could she say those things?' she asked him as he flopped down next to her, 'I'm her family.'

'I don't know. She's torn, I guess. I was talking to Redka, and your mum and Alia have been through a hell of a lot together. Maybe she feels obligated to follow the queen?'

She hunched her shoulders and let her head roll in Connor's direction. 'When did you get so sensible?'

Connor laughed and lay back on the grass; fluffy white clouds drifted overhead before being swallowed up by the orange sky to the west.

'I've always been sensible, you just didn't realise 'cause you were too busy checking out my abs.'

She spluttered and punched him playfully on the arm then settled down next to him on the grass.

'I'm sorry I upset you that day.' He didn't move or look at her but spoke to the sky. 'I enjoyed kissing you.'

A hint of a smile played at the corner of her mouth. 'And I enjoyed being kissed, it's just…'

'I know, you're all googly eyes for Prince Charming now and I don't stand a chance.'

Amber snorted. 'I am *not* all googly-eyed. I was going to say you were right. We had...have, got a lot on our plates at the moment, and I can't get distracted with boys...no matter how great their abs are!'

By her side, Connor chuckled as he slipped his hand in hers and they lay in companionable silence staring up at the blue sky.

'**WHAT COULD** I say?' Myanna paced the bedroom floor as the queen watched from the end of the bed. 'Of course I want to be with them, but things are so different. *I'm* so different. I can't go back to being a teacher at some tiny school, living in a small terraced house with a husband I no longer know.'

'So what are you going to tell her?'

Myanna threw her hands in the air and let out a frustrated cry. 'You didn't see this coming? You said you sensed a warrior who would break the bonds and help us to escape; you didn't see that it was going to be her?'

'My visions aren't as strong as when I am in Avaveil, you know that. I sensed a warrior, yes, and two have arrived. How could I have known Amber was a warrior? She said it herself, her powers were cloaked by a curse, and you never even told me about her oracle heritage.'

'I assumed it wasn't true. My own mother told me that my healing and magic powers were present from birth, but when Amber didn't show any signs at all I assumed the prophecies were untrue or Alan's descendants had lied.'

'You doubted your own husband?'

'No...yes, I wanted my father to be so proud of his granddaughter, the chosen one, the oracle to unite the ancients, but when nothing happened I blamed it on Alan to soften the blow of disappointment my father bequeathed on me.'

'Did Amber tell you that your husband is missing?'

Myanna nodded. 'They were cursed by a necromancer and she's taken him.'

'You are aware that he has probably been taken to the Lost Lands and if Amber intends to find him she will have to cross the borders into the darkness?'

'I know but what can I do? I can't go back – I won't go back. Alia, you are like a sister to me and my place is by your side in Avaveil.'

'I will happily take you with me, Myanna, you know that, but Amber's powers are strong and she is untrained. She needs a mentor and she needs her mother. Think carefully before you decide which gateway you take.'

Chapter 13

The Guardian ceremony was still a night away but the fortress was buzzing with unusual activity. Hushed conversations and extra guards at the main gates had prompted Queen Alia to dispatch one of her staff to spy on General Loso's quarters.

'If he is expecting a visit from his one of his captains, then this will present us with a problem,' she told them. 'The captains travel with their own mini army and our escape is going to be treacherous enough dealing with Loso's army without having to elude two battalions.'

They worked diligently on assembling the supplies they would need and pushed any thoughts of Guardian armies to the back of their minds.

Connor and Amber had been tasked with fetching fresh dressings and herbs from the stores on the north side of the building. As they hurried back to Alia's courtyard, the atmosphere in the stone corridors became oppressive. Crowds of Guardians flooded every doorway and corridor heading to the great hall, their bulk filling every inch of space, leaving Amber feeling claustrophobic.

They ducked into several doorways to avoid being seen. Most of Alia's staff were free to roam at will but any sharp-eyed Guardian would easily realise they were not her usual staff.

As they rounded the last corner, leading to the covered walkway which circled the great hall, Amber bristled at the sight that greeted them.

Silhouettes danced across the bloodstained marble under the flickering light. Hundreds of candles hung from wooden sconces, dripping hot wax on the mosaic floor. The great hall was alive with noise; Guardians ripped at chunks of meat and bread which had been placed on long trestle tables throughout the centre of the hall, and metal clashed with metal as soldiers practised their swordsmanship along the outer ring.

Connor tugged at Amber's sleeve, bundling her along the covered walkway, their simple cloaks pulled tight around their civilian clothes.

With her hood drawn down over her face she hurried towards the huge wooden doors leading to Alia's courtyard. As they passed the marble slabs, the smell of blood was overwhelming, and she skidded to a halt, resting her hands on her knees. Her stomach knotted and her head pounded as her energies built inside her. She closed her eyes and tried to gasp in a lungful of air, but the pictures she could see in her mind sent her pitching forward. She steadied herself on one of the stone pillars and lifted her gaze. Her legs threatened to give way as she saw the boy strapped to the marble slab, and she struggled not to cry out as panic took hold of her.

'BEGIN!' A booming voice silenced the hall, and Amber took a shuddering breath as she glanced in the direction of the throne. General Loso entered with his entourage of personal soldiers. He was humongous, clad from head to foot in black armour with a huge golden phoenix at the centre of his breastplate, a long red cape sweeping behind him as he strode to the throne, then sat down, his red eyes surveying the room.

He flicked his wrist in the direction of the Guardian who watched over the marble tables.

Amber's eyes darted to the boy who lay bare-chested and chained. Flanked by two huge Guardians he looked so frail.

His arms were fastened to the marble with two worn leather belts. In a flash of silver his wrists were slashed and his blood poured freely from the open wounds, spilling into the carved channels cut into the marble to drain away like dirty bath water.

His freshly shaved head rolled to the side, and he locked eyes with Amber, panic and recognition flickering across his face.

'Amber?' His voice was a mere whisper before his eyes rolled back in his head.

Amber clamped her hands over her mouth to stifle the scream that had risen in the back of her throat. She clearly remembered the day when Mrs Cassidy had wandered into the magic shop looking for her son and now here he was, lying in front of her, bleeding out. Fear coated her insides as she watched Carl's every movement with wide eyes.

'BRING FORTH THE BLOOD FOR RENEWAL!' Loso's voice boomed across the silent hall as another soldier stepped forward carrying a glass vial. She watched helplessly as the Guardian inserted a thin needle attached to a clear tube into his artery. Thick black blood began to pump through his veins and orange sparks danced and caressed his torso.

'We have to move,' hissed Connor, pulling on her sleeve.

She stumbled back as Carl's body convulsed, the strange purple tattoo of the Guardians beginning to swirl across his freshly shaved scalp and twist down his neck. He jolted, bracing himself against his restraints, screaming out in agony as his body stretched and his limbs lengthened. His cries echoed off every surface to fill the air. His body writhed and bucked against his bonds until his shoulders began to swell, growing broader, and his chest expanded. Muscles developed along his arms and legs until Carl, who had looked so frail moments ago, resembled a Guardian; a heavyset warrior designed to kill.

The world began to spin and she needed Connor's help to walk; her legs were jelly and her vision was impaired by a veil of hot tears.

They slipped through the courtyard door unseen, and Amber crumpled as the door closed behind her. Collapsing to her knees, she shook violently and wept.

Connor knelt down beside her. 'There was nothing we could do,' he said, stroking her hair.

She looked up into his purple eyes, his fae magic softening her pain. Nodding as she wiped her eyes she said, 'Thank you, Connor, but if I'm going to beat Loso and free my friend then I need to feel the pain.' She shrugged his hand away and felt the sharp sting in her heart once again.

'Amber!' Redka rushed across the courtyard but she held up a hand to stop him.

'No!' She glared at him as he came to a halt. 'She said the ceremony was tomorrow, your mother said...' She spat the words at Redka, her face clouded with rage, before her voice broke.

'She didn't know...' he whispered, avoiding her icy stare. 'She couldn't help it.'

As Amber watched the range of emotions pass across his face, she was filled with a deep sense of foreboding.

Redka looked her in the eye. 'They moved Tom and...Loso took Myanna.'

Amber felt her world begin to slide away from her as she saw Redka spring forward to catch her, then everything went black.

***

A LIGHT breeze caressed her cheek and she feebly shielded her face against the brightness that pressed against her eyelids. A figure stood over her as she tried to break through her dream state.

'You are safe, little eye.' Lavanya's musical voice drifted over her and settled like a comfort blanket.

'I couldn't stop it,' she sniffed. 'Carl...a boy I knew from school, he's gone and Tom's next. I stood by and watched them hurt him, watched him suffer, and I didn't do anything'

Lavanya cradled her as she cried, gently rocking her until Amber was spent.

With an exhausted sigh, Amber looked up into the ancient oracle's face, finding only affection there and no judgement.

'What should I do?'

Lavanya laughed, a beautiful melody which melted some of the ice on Amber's heart.

'You know what to do, tap into your power, little eye. You can see the right path if you concentrate. Remember your lessons; access the chakra point relevant to that which you seek.'

Amber thought back to her lessons with Connor in a tiny shop, in a tiny town. It seemed like a lifetime ago.

Seven chakras, seven powers – she remembered. Strength, elemental magic, leadership, healing, knowledge, sight and her expanded consciousness.

'What do you seek?' Lavanya's voice coaxed as Amber closed her eyes to feel for her powers.

'I need to find my mum and Tom.'

'You know how to find them, little eye.'

She concentrated on her third eye and cloaked herself in the golden light Connor had taught her about. Her hands and feet began to tingle, and she could feel the power coursing up through her. She focused on the seven colours and pushed her mind out to the chakra of knowledge.

A picture formed in her mind, cloudy at first then becoming clearer. A dark room cut out of black stone, the walls damp. She could see figures, two...her mum was there.

She opened her mind wider until she could see the door, then the corridor, wider and wider until she was seeing a map of the labyrinth of corridors.

The colours unravelled. *'I know where they are,'* she yelled.

'Then it's time for you to return, little eye.'

Lavanya pressed a delicate finger to Amber's forehead; everything went black.

IT HADN'T taken long for Connor and Redka to grab their weapons and be waiting by the map table for instructions.

Amber felt a glow of pride in her new abilities as the three of them studied the yellowed paper.

'The stronghold was designed to snare any invaders. The corridors look confusing, but for someone who has grown up running through these halls it's a simple one way in, one way out design.'

'I agree, the dungeon is placed at the furthest point from the entrance so that anyone lucky enough to escape couldn't possibly make it all the way out without a head to head with a few hundred Guardians.'

Amber's gaze flitted between the two as they bent over the map, heads close together as they strategised their rescue plans. Connor pushed his thick hair out of his eyes, tracing a finger along the map with his spare hand. He had bulked up since they had arrived in Phelan. He and Redka had been training constantly in Alia's garden, practising their sword skills and hand to hand combat. He had a wonderful glow about him that made his eyes twinkle. She wondered what India would say if she could see him now, a bold and strong young warrior.

She turned her attention to Redka; he was handsome in every way. His long white hair was braided down his back with leather cord, and he absent-mindedly swung it over his shoulder as he leant in closer to the table. His blue shirt barely concealed the sculpted muscles beneath and Amber felt her cheeks heat up as she let her gaze take in his physique. She always sensed a great pull in her heart whenever they were near each other, as if they were connected by an invisible piece of string.

Amber felt a gentle hand press against the small of her back jolting her out of her daydream state; Alia smiled at her and gently coaxed her away from the boys who were absorbed in their battle plans.

They walked to the open doors leading to the garden; a large stone fountain, surrounded by wildflowers and apple trees, dominated the centre.

'Your mother is very strong, little eye, do not worry for her. She has survived Loso's dungeons many times before.'

Amber was stunned. 'When?'

Alia patted Amber's hand as they both sat on a low stone bench overlooking the forest.

'Many years ago, when your mother first arrived, she withstood General Loso like no other had. He punished her for that by beating her and making her spend a week in the dungeon. On the day of her release, when the Guardians collected her, she was waiting for them, her shoulders back, chin held high, and she walked through the fortress like a princess.' Alia chuckled at the memory. 'Loso was furious, he had wanted to break her spirit but failed, and Loso never fails.'

'What happened?'

'Once a month your mother had to endure two nights in the dungeon without food or water, and once a month she went without question and walked back out again as proud as ever.'

Amber laughed, her heart bursting with pride.

Alia laughed too. 'Loso gave up in the end and chose to ignore her existence instead…until now anyway.'

'So why is he suddenly so interested in my mother again?'

'He isn't, he suspects that something is wrong and senses that I am involved as he shares my blood. He has eyes and ears on our every movement: my court, my servants, Myanna and my son. I believe he senses that we will attempt to escape.'

'You never refer to Mum as one of your servants, why?'

Alia held Amber's hands in her own and gave them a squeeze. 'Your mother saved my life, and she nursed me back to health when I surely would have died. At that time I wanted death, I even begged her to help me, but she wouldn't listen. Her herbal magic is the finest. She watched over Redka during my sickness, she schooled him and taught him her own magic skills until I was strong enough to teach him the way of the fae. She stood up to Loso for me and I will be eternally grateful.'

'For *you*?'

'Yes, he was taking too much of my blood, which was slowly killing me; a very rare phenomenon for a royal fae. She told him to stop or she would poison my blood, which would in turn have poisoned him. He didn't like being told what to do.'

'How do you cope with that evil man taking your blood and forcing you to do spells on those boys?'

Alia bent her head closer to Amber's. 'He soon realised that Myanna wouldn't poison me as we had grown so close, but he did seem to listen to her argument and so he agreed to let her take a smaller amount of my blood when he needed it. Myanna agreed to his deal, even shook on it.' She laughed at the memory. 'What he doesn't know is that she has been taking blood from lavahogs and passing it off as mine.'

Amber's jaw hung open as she looked up at the queen, her face a picture of girlish joy, as if she had just told the story of two friends braiding each other's hair and gossiping about boys.

'But...that means Loso isn't immortal.' The realisation hit her hard: he could be killed.

'Exactly...we knew something was coming. I could feel it in the magic I weave, so we had to prepare. We just didn't realise that the "something" was you.' She smiled again and released Amber's hands to straighten her skirts.

'Redka is quite smitten with you,' she added with a slight smile.

Amber blushed and looked at her feet; her tattered Converse looked odd next to the delicate silver slippers of the queen.

'I sense a connection to him,' she said carefully. 'Ever since he found me in the forest, I feel like I've always known him, like he's a part of me, but I don't understand why.'

'Soulmates come together when they are in need.'

'Oh, we're not soulmates or anything, just friends...'

Alia smiled at her. 'In the human realm a pairing like this can be a true love or a family member, but in Avaveil it is a magical bond; it is someone you have shared many lifetimes with. It simply means that your emotions are linked; he feels your pain and you feel his. Sometimes soulmates never discover where their connections came from. Just understand that Redka is bound to you for as long as you need him.'

Before Amber could ask any more questions, the boys stepped out of the doorway and strode over to where they were sitting. She could feel her cheeks still burning as she sensed Connor staring at her, but when she met his gaze, his eyes had a faraway air about them, like he was looking straight through her at another time and place. His smile faded abruptly and he walked back inside.

Redka cleared his throat. 'We will wait for dusk and then make our way to the dungeon. More shadows to hide in and less Guardians on the prowl.'

Amber nodded and made her excuses to leave. She needed some alone time to gather her thoughts. Being in such close proximity to Redka was addling her brain. She had such strong feelings for him and they confused her. What had Alia meant when she said they were bound to one another? She had a mission, to rescue Tom and her mother and return safely to Hills Heath and join India's search for her dad. Redka's path was a different one from her own; she had even argued with her mother because of it. He was destined to travel to Avaveil with Alia.

She could see no solution. It was obvious to anyone that they weren't meant to be together, they lived in different worlds. He was fae and she was an oracle. Their bond was merely coincidence and a way to join forces to save the people they loved, and yet she couldn't shake the feeling that there was something more, something that was bigger than both of them.

Chapter 14

The shadows of the fortress offered ample hiding places as they wound their way through the labyrinth of tunnels. Cobwebs clung to the low ceilings and danced in the faint breeze as they hurried past. Each passage was cloaked in darkness, the unnatural black candles spaced out far enough to light only a minuscule section at a time.

'How do you not get lost down here?' Connor asked as they passed what he thought was the same statue they had seen ten minutes ago.

Redka's lips curled up in a mischievous smile. 'I spent my childhood following the Guardians through these tunnels, hidden from sight, until I learned where every stone was in this place. The Guardians thought I was an evil spirit, they never did find out it was me.'

Connor snorted.

'My mother told me that a warrior would come to free us and aid our return to Avaveil, so it made sense to familiarise myself with the fortress. Luckily Loso just saw me as an inquisitive child, roaming his corridors and great halls, playing at being a soldier with my wooden swords.'

'Let's hope Lady Luck is on our side today.'

Redka chuckled and carried on down the stone corridor leading to the turret steps. The cells were in the lower section of the rotund building. A spiral staircase directed them to a small hallway where the first of the guards would be posted.

'Ready?'

Amber looked into Redka's purple eyes and nodded. She was shaking inside but there was also a sense of something else – exhilaration. She was actively doing something good, saving her mother and Tom, when she hadn't been able to save Carl from his terrible fate. For a brief moment she also felt a sense of belonging, a belonging to a strange world of fortresses, demons, faeries and Guardians.

'Let's go!'

'**GOOD EVENING**, General Loso, how can I be of service?' Maggie bustled across the courtyard towards the towering bulk of the general, her pink wings fluttering as she walked. His red eyes were fixed on her every move. She kept her chin up and a bright smile on her face as she stopped in front of him.

'Where is Alia?'

'She is resting, General. The unexpected bloodletting took it out of her, and having to perform two protection spells in such a hurry, well she just...'

'Bring her!' His voice remained low, but there was no mistaking his tone, and Maggie curtseyed then hurried through to Queen Alia's rooms.

Alia had sensed his arrival before Maggie could even confirm his presence. She had known he would come for more blood. With Myanna locked up in the cells, she was vulnerable and he revelled in that. They had all counted on it for their plan to work.

She scooped up the glass vial from the table and swirled the blood around several times, then pulling off the stopper, she dropped the ground herbs into the blood, replaced the lid and swirled the contents again. She looked at Maggie, who stood patiently at the door, and smiled.

'It's time.' Maggie nodded and disappeared into the back rooms to collect their belongings as arranged. Alia smoothed her deep green velvet gown and glided to the courtyard door.

'My dear general, I wasn't expecting you until tomorrow evening.' She smiled at him as he bowed in greeting. The strangest combination of murderous warrior and court gentleman, she thought.

'My captains from the south are due here in two days, and I want to ensure I am at full strength.' He glanced at the vial she was holding. 'May I?'

Alia handed over the small object and moved to the seating area. She invited the general to join her as she splayed her skirts around her.

He sat across from her and lay his sword on the long table which separated them. Alia flinched at the sight of it.

Loso's laugh was cold. 'In all these years you have never got used to life in a demon realm, my dear queen.'

'I should hope not, General. A member of fae royalty has no need for such barbaric weaponry…'

'Nonsense!' he bellowed. 'Your own boy is as skilled as any of my soldiers, and is he not in line for the throne of Avaveil?'

A veil of sadness settled over Alia as she looked at the general with glassy eyes. 'My son will never have that opportunity unless you allow us to leave, my dear general.'

Loso stood abruptly and began pacing the room, his heavy black boots scraping on the tiled floor. 'I am not having this discussion with you again, Alia. You need to realise that this is your home now. If only you would accept my proposal, we could be husband and wife and rule this realm together. Your son would be King of Phelan one day.'

Alia shook her head. 'Avaveil is part of my heart and I can never forget it exists, just as my people will never forget that I am their queen.'

He studied her for a long moment. 'Your people have long since given up all hope of your return, my queen. Trust me when I say that Phelan is the only home you have now.'

He took the stopper out of the vial and drained the liquid in one gulp. Alia watched as he swallowed its contents and willed herself to remain calm.

'It will take me some time to think of Phelan as my home, General, and not my prison.'

He sat opposite her once more, his great size filling the ornate chair. He leant forward holding his hands out towards her in an open gesture of hope. 'I only ask that you try, my queen.'

Alia smiled up at the general and nodded. 'As you request, I shall try.'

He squared his shoulders and nodded, satisfied that once again he had managed to manipulate her.

Maggie bustled through the door with a tray of food and two glasses of wine and set them on the table next to the general's sword.

'Bread and cheese, General?'

Loso stood and retrieved his sword. 'Not for me...' He swayed slightly and placed a hand on the back of the chair to steady himself.

'Are you unwell, General?' Maggie peered into his face. 'I can get some herbal tea instead.'

Alia watched the general look from Maggie to the tray and then to the empty vial in his hand. His fiery red eyes settled on Alia, and she was surprised to find hurt and pain there as he registered that the blood was drugged.

He lurched for the courtyard door, but Maggie swung out a foot and he stumbled, lost his footing and careered across the floor, landing heavily in a heap against the far wall.

Maggie checked his breathing and slapped him hard across the face.

'Maggie! Was that absolutely necessary?'

'Sorry, Your Majesty, just wanted to make sure. He's out cold.'

Alia took the gateway key from around his neck and secured the chain over her head before they dragged his body through to her private bedroom and covered him with a pile of blankets.

Straightening her hair and smoothing out her dress, she moved to the main doors. There were two soldiers outside her rooms when she opened them.

'Ah good, General Loso said you would be here. He requires the Avaveil maps from the library and asked that you both hurry and retrieve them for him.'

The two soldiers looked from Alia to one another and back again, their blank faces and fiery eyes giving no indication as to whether they believed her or not.

'What maps?' the one on the left asked.

'The Fae territory, he is thinking of invading and needs my assistance to find the most accessible route.' She held the soldiers' harsh gaze for a long moment.

'Very well,' he said eventually, and the two soldiers moved off in the direction of the library at the other end of the fortress.

Alia exhaled loudly and closed the door behind her. Resting her back against the wood she prayed that Redka, Connor and Amber made it back in time, before the guards returned from their false trail.

***

AS GRAND entrances went, Amber thought that this one could have gone better. The soldier left to guard the prisoners lay at Redka's feet with a gaping wound in his chest, his last breath leaving him as Redka frisked his immense frame for the cell key.

'Did you have to kill him?'

Redka unhooked the key from the soldier's belt. 'Yes, if he had lived he would have raised the alarm and then killed all of us.'

'What is it, Amber?' Connor laid a hand on her shoulder. 'You're trembling.'

'The soldiers, Guardians, whatever you want to call them...they were once boys, just like you and Carl and Tom. I just didn't think we would be killing them all.'

'They *were* like us, but no more. The ceremony strips them of all their humanity. They don't remember being a boy, they only remember wanting to hunt and kill.'

She knew he was right, but the dead Guardian at their feet could easily have been Carl or Dan or any boy from Hills Heath.

The screech of the cell doors' hinges stirred her from her thoughts. The heavy door swung wide and in the doorframe stood Myanna, her long navy dress filthy and torn, her face smeared with blood and dirt, but in her arms she held a thin figure with a mop of dirty blond hair.

'Tom!' Amber flew forward and enveloped her friend in a tight embrace. She could feel his weak arms encircle her and hug her back.

'Hey, cutie,' he murmured in her ear, his voice croaky from lack of water. 'Thanks for stopping by.'

Amber laughed and clung to her best friend, relief and happiness mixing with her fears.

'I was so worried that I wouldn't see you again.'

She swallowed down her shock at how gaunt and ashen he looked. His perfectly styled hair stood in grimy tufts around his head, and his clothes hung off his wasted frame, shredded and dirty.

'Your mum wants to know if you'll be home for tea,' she said softly.

Tom laughed and winced as it caused him pain. 'That would be nice but only if she's not serving custard, I've gone off that all of a sudden.'

Amber giggled and patted him on the shoulder affectionately. 'I'll have a quiet word, she'll understand.'

※

GETTING BACK to the court was a long and tedious journey. Tom was weak from lack of food and water and Myanna had sustained an injury to her knee when the Guardians had dragged her down the stone steps to the cells.

Amber half carried, half dragged Tom as they followed Redka through the winding corridors. They were making slow progress. Connor glanced back at her as he helped Myanna. His eyes said it all – they were running out of time.

※

ALIA WASN'T used to pacing. She was a queen and royalty didn't pace. Maggie on the other hand was used to pacing and kept up an almost hypnotic rhythm next to her.

'Something's wrong,' she muttered, more to herself than to Maggie.

'Don't fret, Your Majesty, they'll be here.'

The doors leading to the walled garden stood open letting the cool night air circulate within the room. Both Alia and Maggie were already in their travelling clothes, with dark green hooded capes and cloth bags holding all the food they could carry for the journey. They had purposefully made each of the bags as light as they could. It was going to be tough enough to climb down the face of the mountain without a heavy bag to hinder anyone's progress.

The door to the courtyard swung open and Redka staggered through supporting Myanna with one hand, as she used a sword as a walking stick. Connor followed and Amber came last, clinging to a frail blond boy. She slammed the door shut as the boy she was holding slumped to the floor with a gasp.

'The effort of walking so far has been too much,' Redka addressed his mother, his purple eyes wide with an unspoken fear. Alia nodded her understanding.

'It is going to get worse before it gets better my friends.' She knelt down and caressed Tom's cheek with her hand. 'We need you to be strong for a little while longer. There is a dangerous journey ahead of us, but beyond that is home…' Her voice drifted off to nothing, leaving an aura of hope hanging in the air.

Tom nodded and with Amber's help he got back to his feet. 'I want to go home ma'am, whatever it takes.'

Alia smiled at him. 'This may help a little, open your mouth slightly.' She placed her hands around his face, and Amber watched in awe as wisps of golden light left Alia's open mouth and drifted into Tom's.

'What's she doing?' Amber asked Redka as he secured a cloth bag to his back.

'She is sharing some of her magic to give him strength.'

The door to Alia's private room smashed open and splintered as it hit the wall. The small group spun round and saw General Loso burst through the opening, his sword drawn.

'What a touching scene,' he spat. 'But I'm afraid I haven't finished with any of you yet.'

Redka and Connor drew their swords.

The general growled. 'How our little prince has grown.'

He glared at Redka with pure hatred burning in his ruby eyes.

'I'm taking my mother out of Phelan, General, and you aren't going to stop me.'

'That remains to be seen, my dear prince.' He lost his balance briefly but supported himself against the wall. 'Your mother drugged me and...' He lunged at Alia and snatched the gateway key from around her neck, '...stole from me. She needs to be punished. Maybe I could start by slicing sweet Myanna's head off.'

'Leave my mother alone!' Amber straightened, still holding Tom's arm and stared into the fiery eyes of the general who towered above any of them.

'Mother! How interesting. I do like a girl with fire,' Loso said vehemently. 'Maybe I'll let Myanna watch as I slice off *your* head.' He licked his lips and took a step forward.

Connor and Redka reacted at the same moment and raised their swords to bar his advance, protecting the group who stood behind them. Protecting Amber.

'You will never lay a finger on my daughter, Loso.' Myanna moved quickly, and putting all of her weight behind her, swung the sword she had taken off the fallen guard in the cell and released it. It flew through the air and struck Loso in the side. He roared and fell back through the open doorway, landing on the floor with a loud crack.

'Run!' Myanna herded everyone outside and to the walled garden. 'He won't stay down for long.'

One by one they swung over the wall and scrambled down the jagged rock face of the fortress. The sound of General Loso calling his guard reverberated into the night sky above them as they descended into the forest.

Chapter 15

The black rocks tore at their clothing as they climbed down the mountain to the ground. The shouts and cries of the Guardians from the fortress hung in the air around them. Amber stayed close to Tom, helping him manoeuvre his way over the rocks. His breath was coming fast and shallow and his skin was as pale as the moons which hung above them in the night sky.

'Give me your hand.' Connor held his hand out for Amber. He had made it to the bottom first and was guiding everyone down the last of the rocks.

Amber squeezed his hand tightly as she jumped to the ground before helping Tom down the last few feet.

'We don't have much time, Loso's troops have been dispatched and they will be swarming the forests soon. We will make for the gateway to the north.' Redka led the small group into the forest.

Tom winced with every step as they rushed through the trees. Myanna wasn't doing much better, and Amber could see the pain etched on her mother's face every time she placed her foot on the floor.

'Can't we let them rest for just a few minutes?' She had caught up to Redka and was keeping pace with him, leaving Connor to prop Tom up.

'If we stop they will find us. The only advantage we have is a head start and that will lessen once Loso's soldiers fill the forest. He won't stop until we are all caught, and I don't even want to think of the consequences.'

Amber nodded. 'You're right, we can rest once we get to Hills Heath.'

Redka glanced across at Amber briefly. 'When we reach the gateway we will have no time for goodbyes, Amber. You will need to make your way through the tunnel as quickly as possible and we will need to press forward to reach the faerie ring in the south. My mother's powers are already waning, and she will get weaker with every step we take away from the fortress.'

'I don't understand, I thought my mother healed her all those years ago.'

'She did but her powers were concentrated only on the fortress. Once she leaves the prison her fae powers will weaken quickly. This is why I must get her to Avaveil as quickly as possible.'

Amber glanced at the queen and watched as she helped Myanna over a fallen tree. They clung to one another like frightened children. Although Alia was still as beautiful, she noticed a grey pallor to her skin and a paleness to her wings.

'What will happen if she loses her powers?'

'It's already happening.' Redka nodded his head to the left; through the trees Amber could see the faint orange glow of fire. Where the trees once stood there was now an outcrop of black rock surrounded by a pool of lava. Amber gasped.

'You remember the true face of Phelan you saw when you looked through the window? The elemental changes that my mother placed on the landscape are being stripped away, and all this beauty will soon become rock and fire again.'

Running from the Guardians was hard enough, but managing the terrain of Phelan would be near impossible for the small group. Tom was weak and slow, and her mother was injured and struggling to keep up with the swift pace.

'I can help,' she said suddenly, as if the right path had always been there but she hadn't noticed. 'I can cause a distraction and keep the Guardians busy while we escape.'

Redka looked on curiously. 'What do you have in mind?'

Connor herded Tom, Myanna and Maggie to a safe distance while Redka carved out a protective circle into the moss-covered floor.

Alia stood inside the circle holding Amber's hands in her own.

'This may just work, little eye,' she said, smiling through her obvious discomfort. Her magic was failing quickly and if they didn't act soon, there may be nothing left for Amber to tap into.

'Call to the Dragovax,' Amber told her. 'Help me draw them out.'

The air in the forest became very still and there were no sounds to be heard aside from the gentle breathing of the two figures in the centre of the circle.

A golden glow surrounded them and inched slowly away, creeping over the ground, sending slivers of light out into the darkness. A loud screech filled the air to the north and another to the west. The Dragovax had heard their call and they were coming.

Tom bent his head closer to Connor. 'If this works won't all the demons in the area head our way?'

Connor nodded. 'I think that's the idea. They'll answer the call, but hopefully we won't be here, and all they'll find are our Guardian friends who, might I add, invaded their homeland, so big battle ensues and we escape unseen – in theory.'

'In theory,' Tom repeated quietly.

Alia slumped forward as the elemental spell took its toll, and Amber caught her before she fell, breaking the connection between them.

'It worked,' she said. 'I feel them drawing closer.'

'Then it's time for us to leave.' Redka stepped forward and lifted his mother out of Amber's arms. He wrapped an arm around her waist and helped her as they moved off into the ever decreasing forest terrain.

Black rocks jutted up from the ground as more and more trees turned to dust around them. A choking heat rose up from the floor as they moved without making a sound. Howls and screams filled the night air behind them, and the sounds of raised voices chased them on the breeze.

They reached the caves as the last of the trees burned, the moss and the tiny wildflowers withering to ash. The terrain was harsh, fire spewed from in between the rocks, and the sky glowed orange for as far as the eye could see. They made their way wordlessly through the cave until they reached the wall of flames.

'We will rest briefly while you make contact with your coven.' He let his shoulders drop. 'I'm sorry, Amber, but then we must leave you.'

'I know.' She felt a heavy knot form in her chest as she said the words. This was the end of their brief friendship; their respective worlds were calling to them. It was time to break that bond, but she didn't know if she possessed the strength to walk away.

She looked at Tom who was slumped against the wall with his head resting on his knees. He needed her to get him safely home. Myanna sat with Maggie and the queen in a small huddle as Maggie applied a healing salve to her knee. The pull on her heartstrings was suffocating. Myanna still hadn't decided if she was going with her or Alia. There was every possibility that her heart was about to get torn into tiny pieces by two of the most important people in her life and she wasn't even remotely prepared for it.

Connor broke away from the group, and tearing the pendant from his pack, he channelled his energy into the flat crystal. Amber joined him as its colour shifted and swirled. Connor tensed beside her.

'What it is?'

'Something's wrong.'

They peered at the stone's surface as it swirled from a deep purple and finally cleared. They could see the storeroom clearly and the charred remains of a pentagram. India's face drifted into view.

'Connor, I'm so sorry.'

'We don't have the key, drop the wall, Indi.' Amber's voice rose slightly as panic began to set in. She felt it too, something was terribly wrong.

'We can't drop the gateway.' Tears rolled down India's face as she delivered the blow. 'The gateway was guarded and we couldn't hold it, the phoenix was just too strong...Lydia is dead.'

Amber felt a numbness rise up from her feet despite the heat in the stones she stood on. They were trapped, with no way home, surrounded by demons and Guardians in a valley of flames.

'We tried to do the spell with just the three of us but it didn't work, I'm so sorry.'

Connor's hands shook as he held the pendant. 'We'll find another way, Indi, don't worry.'

'How?' Amber snapped. 'That's the only way home, Connor. Loso has the key and he's out there hunting us, we're trapped here.'

'The faerie ring,' he said, closing his eyes. 'Get Redka, tell him everything that's happened, we may be able to use it to get home.'

Amber's heart hammered in her chest as she lurched off in the direction of the small group. Redka was checking Myanna's knee when she approached. Her mother smiled up at her, but her face froze as she looked at her daughter's expression.

'What is it, Amber?'

'There's been an accident...one of the coven has been killed and they can't drop the gateway. We need to find another way. Can I speak with Redka for a moment?'

He stood and followed Amber to the far side of the cave, the shadows shielding them from the rest of the group as she placed her hand on his arm. 'We were wondering about the faerie ring. Could we use it to get home?'

Redka's purple eyes fixed on Amber's and she felt her panic lessen slightly. His hypnotic gaze filled her with a floating sensation, and she had to shake her head to clear her mind.

'The faerie ring can't take you home, Amber, it will only take you to Avaveil. It may be wise to take this option and work out an alternative route home from my homeland.'

Amber's heart rate quickened, maybe this wasn't goodbye after all.

Redka continued, 'The ring will work, but I can't guarantee we will make it there in one piece.'

His eyes wavered and for the first time Amber could see the distress in them. Worry for the queen, fear for the group and the fear of a greater loss that overwhelmed all of his other worries.

'We can do this,' she said in a small voice. 'Together we can get them through.'

He wrapped his arms around her and pulled her close, heat flooding through her veins as she breathed in his scent: jasmine and the deep woody tang of the earth. She didn't care if it was his fae powers at work or her oracle ones. She felt whole, she felt like she belonged here, wrapped in his arms.

He began to pull away but she hung on to him, keeping him close as she looked up into his beautiful face. The curve of his nose, the length of his eyelashes and the sensuous shape of his mouth were all carefully catalogued and stored in her heart. His eyes moved over her face as if he was also committing her features to memory. He leant down and gently brushed his lips against hers, everything went silent, and nothing else existed apart from him. She kissed him back, with the urgency and despair she felt coursing through her, and he clung to her, winding his hand in her hair. They were surrounded by silence, cocooned in their own passion, oblivious to everything else around them. He slipped his tongue inside her mouth and she groaned. Her heart beat quickened and she longed to stay in his embrace forever. Too soon he pulled away. 'I can't lose you,' he breathed into her, hair sending an electrical current up her spine.

She trailed her thumb across his lips.

'You won't lose me, not now, not ever.' He was all she wanted and the thought of being without him was too much to bear. They had to find a way, a way to search for her dad and still be together.

***

AMBER FOUND Connor staring into the wall of flames, a mask of pain on his face.

'We need to move.' She placed a hand on his shoulder, 'Redka said the faerie ring will only get us to Avaveil, but that's a better place to find our way home from than Phelan is right now.'

He nodded and as she moved to walk away he grabbed her by the hand and pulled her close, his face bent towards hers. For a brief moment she thought he was going to kiss her.

'Whatever happens, I want you to know I'll always be here for you.'

'Thank you, Connor.'

'I mean it, this journey is going to be hard, we will have to make some tough decisions, and I want you to know I've got your back.'

She wrapped her arms around his neck and gave him a tight hug.

'Come on, let's get this lot out of here and pay Tinkerbell a visit.' They smiled at each other and some of the tension lifted. As she twisted her head to look for Tom she saw her mother studying her. Amber couldn't swallow down the unease that had crept into the pit of her stomach. For now they were together, but Myanna's inability to choose between Amber and her loyalty to the queen hung over them like a brewing storm.

Chapter 16

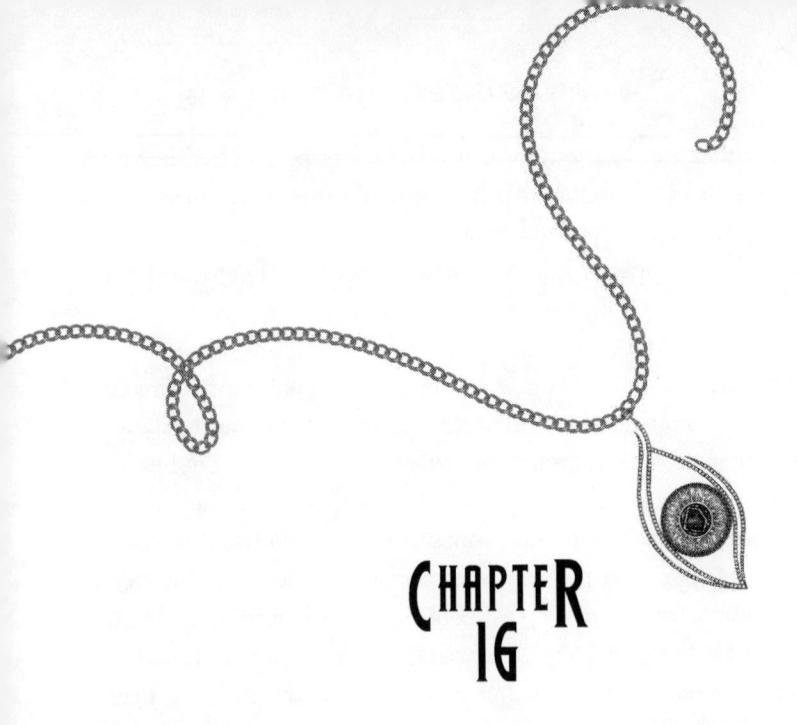

Redka led the small group back out of the cave. They headed south keeping to the shadows of the craggy rocks. The landscape was bereft of all of Alia's elemental magic. Her powers had drained much faster after they performed the spell to call the Dragovax.

From the screams and roars drifting from the west, Amber knew the spell had worked; the sounds of battle rang in the air.

'Let's hope the demons keep them busy long enough to give us time to reach the faerie ring,' Connor mumbled.

Tom lost his footing on the uneven rock, and both Amber and Connor reached out to stop him falling. 'Thanks.' He gave them a lopsided grin. 'Can I ask you guys a question? I understand that the fiery cave we just left was our only way home, so why are we heading to this faerie ring?'

'The gateway can only be opened by a key, which Loso has, or by four coven witches, and now Lydia has gone, they can't do the spell we need,' Connor explained.

'Yeah, I get that, but what's stopping Loso and his army of brutal soldiers from using the key and walking straight into Hills Heath to massacre everyone in the town?'

Amber stopped dead and looked at him with wide eyes, 'I didn't even think about that, he's so angry with us that he might just burn our home to the ground as revenge.'

Redka appeared at her side and ushered her to keep walking. 'The key is a powerful amulet and Loso has used it to access many realms. Each realm usually has its own gateway and key, unique to that particular land, but Loso's key can grant him access to any realm. I don't think he would concentrate his efforts on destroying your realm, even if he is out for revenge. It's Avaveil that would be in peril as we have taken the queen.'

'Don't we need this key to get through your faerie gateway?' Tom asked.

'No, I have made this gateway in secret, it doesn't need a key so we will need to destroy it once we are all safely through.'

'If we use the faerie ring to escape, aren't we just going to end up even further away from home?'

'The faerie ring will take us to Avaveil,' Redka explained. 'This is my homeland. My people will help us find a way to get you home, Tom, do not fear.'

'Does your homeland have an army of evil soldiers looking to skin us all alive?'

Redka laughed. No, my friend, Avaveil is a peaceful realm full of beauty and colourful characters – or so my mother tells me.'

'You've never been to your own homeland?'

'I was born in Phelan, my mother was taken from Avaveil when she was pregnant, so any memories are what my mother has shared with me, but trust me, Tom, it is much better than here.'

Tom laughed. 'There can't be anywhere worse than here!'

'Tell me more about the gateways,' Amber said as she fell into step beside Redka.

'Phelan's gateway as you know is made of fire; our faerie ring will transport us to Avaveil's gateway which is an ancient oak tree in the west woods. The oak is cloaked in elemental magic and moves to conceal its position.'

'Clever, but doesn't that mean we could end up anywhere in Avaveil when we arrive?'

'It does, but my mother will be able to guide us to the castle.'

'Are there other realms?'

'There are many: the dragon realm, the Lost Lands, each has a unique gateway, one which Loso's key can access.'

'He could invade any realm then?'

'Yes, his own lands were plundered many thousands of years ago which is what drove him to Phelan. Why he chose this place I don't know but it has served him well. None of the other great realm leaders had any desire for this place, leaving him alone for centuries to build an army.'

'Maybe that was his plan all along: build his army in secret and then conquer the other realms. Your own people couldn't find your mother when she was taken prisoner, so he has the perfect hiding place.'

'What are you saying, Amber?'

'I'm saying that it isn't just the human and fae realms that are in danger. Once the others are safely through your faerie ring we may have to think seriously about staying behind to find that key.'

All three boys began talking at once, their voices raised.

'No way, we are getting you to safety,' Connor cried.

'We must leave, we can work out a plan from Avaveil and utilise my mother's armies but we *are* leaving this place, Amber.'

'Cutie, now is not the time for heroics.' Tom's warm eyes held hers as she nodded at him.

'I know you're all right, but Loso is more dangerous than any of us realise and we do need to stop him.'

'We aren't disputing that, Amber,' Connor said softly, 'but let's stop him once we have our own army, when we are better equipped and maybe after a hot bath and bowl of stew.'

She laughed. 'That does sound better actually.'

Alia called out from up ahead, interrupting their discussion. They had arrived at the faerie ring.

Amber didn't know what she had been expecting a faerie ring to look like, but a simple circle of stones wasn't it. She had been about to ask Redka if this was it when she saw Queen Alia praise him for his work and realised that this plain-looking circle was also cloaked in elemental magic.

She closed her eyes and concentrated her own powers, grounding and shielding herself then sending her energies to her third eye chakra. When she finally opened her eyes she gasped; the circle of stones glowed a deep purple. A curtain of silver stars shot up into the sky from the ground, shimmering and swirling as the magic coursed through it. It was the most incredible thing Amber had ever seen.

Redka was organising everyone into groups. 'Only two people at a time can travel through the portal, so we will do this in stages. I haven't had time to test this, so let's pray that it works and doesn't rip us all into a million pieces or leave us floating in some in-between realm for all eternity.'

'Is that a possibility?' Tom asked as he eyed the circle of stones suspiciously.

'Don't worry, Tom, I'll be right beside you.' Myanna wrapped her arm around his waist and squeezed.

'Thanks, Mrs N.'

MAGGIE AND Alia went first, sending one of Alia's silver slippers back through the gateway to prove it had worked and they weren't floating in nowhere land. With great relief etched on Tom's drawn features, he and Myanna went next.

Amber clung to Tom before he stepped through the silver curtain.

'I will be right behind you, Tom,' she told him. 'You will be perfectly safe with Mum.' She turned to her mother and gave her a tight hug. 'Take care of each other and I will see you soon.'

'Chill out, cutie, I've coped all this time without you, I'm sure another sixty seconds won't kill me.'

She gave him a mock frown then sent him through the gateway.

Connor stepped forward and looked at the circle of stones, 'Amber, are you coming?' he held out his hand to escort her through into the circle. Instinctively she stepped back but regretted her action as she saw the pain ghost across his face.

'You go ahead,' she said. 'We'll bring up the rear.'

He looked at her for a long moment before stepping into the silver curtain without another word. She felt a pain shoot through her chest as she watched the magic energy swallow him whole.

'Are you ready?' she asked Redka, eager to get out of Phelan and leave the black rocks behind.

'Almost.' He looked around the floor until he found the cloth sack he had been carrying. 'Nearly forgot our supplies, we don't want to reach Avaveil without the ingredients for Connor's stew now, do we?'

Amber laughed and waited by the silver curtain. She could feel the power coursing through it as the magic tore a hole in reality. It really was an amazing creation, and she pondered how many years Redka had been building this in secret.

A loud demonic roar filled the air and Amber whirled to look for Redka. 'We have to move, *now!*'

She glanced in the direction of the demon's roar and then back to where Redka was retrieving his cloth sack. He faltered, a look of complete horror and shock carved across his handsome features.

Amber watched as the sack slipped from his grasp and he pitched to his knees, a silver blade protruding from his chest.

As he sank to the floor, blood gushing from his wound, a golden phoenix filled her vision and Loso's immense frame stepped into view from behind Redka's fallen body.

'NO!' she screamed, rushing forward just as Loso pulled the sword free and Redka collapsed to the floor.

'You foolish girl, did you think I would just let you walk out of my realm? I have built an empire here among the rocks, an army who follows my every command and I am IMMORTAL!' his voice boomed across the rocky terrain, flames rising higher from the open craters which encircled the faerie ring.

Amber broke down in tears as she knelt on the floor and cradled Redka's body. His breathing was shallow and he was losing blood from the stab wound. Her heart thundered in her chest and she coughed as the heat from the flames intensified.

'I will not allow you to die in this hellhole,' she told him, kissing his forehead and intertwining her fingers with his. 'Don't you dare die on me, Redka, we are bound together.'

His body jerked uncontrollably and he let out a strangled cry, his head rolled to the side and his fingers fell from her grasp as his body grew limp in her arms.

A sudden overwhelming rage swept through her as she carefully lowered his head to the floor. She stood to face Loso, her eyes cold and hard. The energy rose up from her feet, pouring into every fibre of her body until it vibrated through to her bones, stronger than she had ever felt before. With her hands held out to the side she channelled all her power to her sacral chakra, deep in her belly. She could sense her own emotions beginning to take over: her rage, grief and anger coursing through her with an unquestionable thirst for revenge.

The ground around them began to shake as she pulled even more power from the earth. Craters opened up around them and hot molten lava spewed out of the tops, the sky rumbled and fiery bolts of lightning cracked above them.

'How are you doing this?' Loso shouted above the noise, his face showing the first signs of fear as the ground beneath him bucked and twisted. 'You're just a girl.'

Amber's lips pulled back over her teeth in a feral snarl. 'How wrong you are, General.'

He leapt to the side as the earth sliced open, coughing up balls of fire.

Amber's hands glowed a deep orange and small flames licked the surface of her arms and clothes. The fire circled her like a cloak, whipping her hair around her face, but the inferno didn't burn, it caressed her and moved as one with her. She lifted her arms skywards and the winds rose and tore at the black rocks, showering Loso with debris as he shielded his immense bulk.

Amber walked forward, her hands still held out as she channelled all her rage into the storm she rained down on him. She kicked his sword away and stood over him, chanting under her breath as words poured into her from an unknown entity. Something caught her eye and she leant down to snatch the pendant from his neck.

He kicked out with his heavy boot and sent her crashing to the floor, her power snapping back inside her like an elastic band. With the wind knocked out of her, Loso was quick to regain his composure and snatch up his sword.

He struck her hard across the cheek with the back of his hand as she tried to scramble to her feet. She hit the ash-covered floor hard and rolled onto her back just as he raised the tip of his sword to her throat. She crawled backwards over the ground, slicing her hands open on the rocks as she went.

He leered at her as she came to a stop by Redka's body.

'You are all alone, little girl, your friends have abandoned you, your prince is dead. You belong to me now.'

As he pulled his arm back to strike her she closed her eyes tightly and clung to Redka's broken body, but the blow didn't come and she slowly opened her eyes.

A Dragovax held Loso aloft by the throat, its claws digging into his flesh as dark black liquid spilled down his armour. Its rancid teeth were showing, stained with blood from a fresh kill.

'I am immortal!' boomed Loso as he sliced wildly at the creature with his sword.

'No, General, you aren't.' Amber stood on shaky legs, keeping a wary eye on the mountainous creature that held Loso in a vice-like grip. 'My mother has tricked you for many years and the blood that runs in your veins is not immortal fae blood but the blood of lavahogs.'

His fiery red eyes grew wide as her revelation hit home, and he struggled against the demon's grip, twisting to try to free himself.

Amber stumbled backwards as more Dragovax demons approached, their attention captured by the general as he flailed his arms and legs.

She reached down for Redka, keeping a watchful eye on the demons. Grabbing his arms she dragged his body in the direction of the circle of stones. There was no way she was leaving him in Phelan.

Loso roared as he cut at the demon holding him, causing it to drop him to the ground.

Amber screamed as he grabbed her by the hair and pulled her away from the gateway. Redka's body hovered on the edge of the ring, blood pooling around his fallen body. Loso tossed Amber to the floor and she rolled over the dusty ground, crashing into the black rocks. She leapt to her feet and watched as Loso kicked Redka hard in the stomach, his cruel laugh reverberating off the black rocks. 'Your broken little prince is worthless now.'

A deep growl bubbled up from the back of her throat. Her vision was hazy from the blood that was pouring from a cut above her eye. She let her gaze rest briefly on Redka's body, lying still and bleeding at Loso's feet. With absolute clarity she knew that she loved him, and that she now had the power to rip the world in two if she had to live without him. She readied herself for Loso's attack, and her power rushed forward as she pulled it from the ground. She sent columns of fire up from the craters. Her grief and anger took over and the pain she felt coursed through her veins unguarded. Somewhere in a detached part of her mind she could sense Lavanya calling to her, but her raw emotions had taken control. Her body was a living flame, consumed by magic. She pulled her hands back and threw the fire that surrounded her at the general. It hit him square in the chest and he screamed as the flames engulfed him, the smell of burning flesh filling the air.

Lavanya's musical voice called to her again, a sound so far away that it seemed to be coming down to her from the heavens, calling for her to stop, to return to herself before she was overcome by magic. Amber heard her sweet voice and clung to it with her mind, pulling herself back from the red rage that surrounded her, hanging on to every syllable, every sentence until the world came rushing back to her. She collapsed to the floor as the world spun black and orange around her. The demons surged forward and surrounded Loso, his cries and screams filling the air as they tore him apart.

Resisting the urge to vomit, she ran to Redka's side and grabbed at his shirt. She hoisted him into a sitting position, her arms hooked under his armpits as he let out a soft cry.

'Redka, oh, thank God you're alive, please hold on for me, I'm taking you home.'

With a final look at the frenzied mass of demons ripping into Loso's body, she dragged Redka across the stone circle and through the silver curtain.

Chapter 17

It felt like she was being submerged in very deep water, that strange sensation when your ears fill and everything sounds muffled and far away. The wormhole between realms threatened to tear Redka from her arms as it whipped past them. Her chest felt tight and she struggled for air.

Redka's face was colourless and he felt cold in her grasp. She hung on to him as they spun through the silver stream of magic, holding his body close to her, her chest pressing against the wound in his back and her hand held tightly over the wound in his chest, blood seeping through her fingers as she spoke gently into his ear.

'Stay with me, Redka, you are nearly home. Stay with me.'

She kissed his hair and his cheek repeatedly. 'Don't leave me, Redka,' she sobbed, 'I love you.'

Like a cork erupting from a champagne bottle they burst out onto a grassy clearing. She shook her head, trying to clear the nauseous sensation that overwhelmed her from travelling through the portal. She was aware of people running towards them as she screamed.

CONNOR PULLED her away from Redka, but she wriggled out of his grasp, kicking and shouting to be set free. Alia and her mother bent over Redka's body, stripping away his clothing to get a better look at his wounds as Maggie pulled dressings and herbs from a cloth sack.

Amber still couldn't hear clearly; her head was fuzzy and her vision swam as she tried to get loose from Connor's vice-like grip.

Tom's face filled her view; he was talking, shouting at her, yet she couldn't make it out. She studied his lips, trying to understand the words, but everything was clouded and she resumed her struggles until Tom slapped her hard across the face.

There was a loud pop in her ears and the world came rushing forward. She could hear the urgency in her mother's voice and the soft encouragement from Alia. There was a running stream somewhere to her left, and she could make out Connor's laboured breathing in her ear.

She stopped struggling, gaping at Tom whose face was flushed under the dirt and grime coating his skin.

'Sorry, cutie, but you were getting kinda hysterical.'

She sagged in Connor's arms and he lowered her to the floor, cradling her in his arms. Tom knelt beside them.

'Where are you hurt, Amber?'

'N...not hurt, I'm fine.'

'You're covered in blood, and you have a gash by your eye, are you sure you aren't hurt?'

'I hit my head, but the blood...it's not mine, its Redka's,' She looked down at her blood-soaked clothing. 'Loso caught up with us and stabbed him before we could make it to the circle.'

The boys stared at her in disbelief. 'How the hell did you get out of there?'

Amber pictured the fire and brimstone she created with her own bare hands, the winds and the sky raining down upon them as she fought against Loso and her own magic, and decided not to tell them the whole story. Not yet.

'The Dragovax turned up and Loso fought with them, I used that cover to escape but not before I saw him ripped apart.'

'Loso's dead?'

'Yes, he's dead,' she said, her voice flat, and then remembering the pendant she took from him, she fished it out of her pocket and held it in the palm of her hand.

'I managed to take this prior to the demons' attack.'

They looked at the gateway key in her hand; it was a tarnished bronze circular object, covered in tiny symbols which looked like runes. There were two sides fitted together with a clasp on the top and a bronze rod with four ornate teeth on the end.

'So the key to every otherworldly realm looks like…a pocket watch?'

Amber shrugged her shoulders. There was no denying that the object was very fifteenth century, but when she opened the clasp there was no clock face. The inside was smooth and the only inscription was two interlocking ovals with a single lapis lazuli crystal at the centre.

'How does it work?' Tom asked as he turned it over to look at the underneath.

'I have no idea.'

Alia called out for Amber who stuffed the object back in her pocket and scrambling to her feet rushed to Redka's side.

'He is very weak but alive. Thank you, Amber, you saved his life.'

Amber stroked her hand across his forehead and hair, and his eyelids fluttered as if he were dreaming.

'Is he conscious?' she asked, looking up into her mother's eyes.

'No, I made a tonic to put him into a comatose state so we could move him without causing him distress. His fae blood will begin to heal his wound as we make our way to the castle, but he will be unconscious for a while.'

Amber nodded and stroked Redka's forehead lightly with her fingertips.

'You did a brave thing, Amber, and I am so proud of you.' Her mother pulled her close and she melted into her arms. Myanna hugged her, rocking her back and forth and smoothing down her hair and Amber never wanted to venture from her protective embrace again.

THEY TOOK it in turns to carry Redka on a makeshift stretcher. The terrain was tricky as the west woods were so tightly-packed with trees of every variety imaginable. Great oaks, slim beeches and towering pines stood shoulder to shoulder and Amber could only see the blue sky fleetingly between the leaves.

They manoeuvred the stretcher over a fallen tree stump and came to a stop in a small clearing.

'We should rest here,' Alia said, laying her cloth sack on the floor. 'There is a woodland village just beyond the treeline, I know the fae lord and he will be happy to assist us.'

'I'll come with you.' Connor broke away from the group to stand by Alia, 'If Redka can't come with you, then I would be honoured to be his stand-in until he recovers.'

'Thank you, Connor.'

She gave instructions to Myanna and Maggie to set up camp and busy themselves with building a fire and fetching water, before moving over to where Amber was sitting holding Redka's hand.

'I know that my son is in safe hands with you, Amber.' She knelt down and kissed him on the forehead then disappeared into the dense forest with Connor following close behind.

Tom flopped down on the mossy floor next to her and bit into an apple. 'So, cutie, how long are you planning on staying in faerie land?' he asked between chews.

'What do you mean?' She knew exactly what he meant. They hadn't been best friends forever for her not to understand the silent question hidden in his words.

He gave her one of his trademark looks and she caved.

'I don't know, Tom, I can't leave until I know Redka is okay or is at least awake. But I feel awful that I'm leaving my dad vulnerable at home with Patricia.'

'Didn't Connor say that his aunt and the coven were helping to find your dad? Maybe they have him wrapped in a blanket on that green sofa in the magic shop sipping herbal tea.'

She laughed. 'I really can't picture my dad and India sipping tea together wrapped in blankets, and he loathes all that hocus pocus.'

'I seem to remember a day when you used to feel the same.'

She looked up at him. His bright blue eyes had regained some of their sparkle and although he was still painfully thin he looked more like his old self.

'How did we get here, Tom?'

'Well...' he paused for dramatic effect, 'I was kidnapped by an evil Guardian, you foolishly followed, dragging the hot guy from the magic shop along for the ride and picking up another equally hot guy en route before storming a fortress, finding your mother and pulling off a daring rescue...have I missed anything out?'

She snorted and playfully punched him on the arm. 'I know how we got *here*.' She motioned at the forest and Redka's sleeping form. 'I mean how did we end up believing in magic and faeries and other realms? I work in a coffee shop on the high street, you play on your Xbox, twenty-four-seven. Aren't we in way over our heads here?'

'I get it, you're scared, so am I, but don't you feel that?' He patted his hand over his heart.

'What?'

'I really thought I was going to die in that fortress, and as I sat rotting in the cell waiting to be turned into one of those red-eyed freaks, I realised that I've wasted my life.'

'You're sixteen, Tom, not forty.'

'I know, I know, but what have I done so far? I barely scraped a decent grade at school, the only thing I enjoy is gaming, which is unfortunately not on the curriculum for A Level study, so I've chosen subjects I loathe, and I moan about it to you because my parents never bother to stop and listen to me.'

'So what are you saying?'

'I'm saying that I feel like I belong here in this freaky world with a band of faeries and my oracle best friend. I feel alive for the first time ever.'

'We have to go home sometime, Tom.'

'Do we?'

She looked into his eyes and realised he wasn't joking. If Tom didn't want to leave and Myanna was still torn between leaving her fae family and reuniting her human family, then what was stopping her from staying here in Avaveil?

She rested her head against his shoulder. 'I do feel it…here.' She patted her own chest. 'But my dad needs me and as soon as we've made sure Redka has recovered then we *will* be going back to Hills Heath – together.'

He rolled his eyes and tossed the apple core into the woods.

'Maybe you could write your own gaming program and battle the Guardians online?' she laughed. 'It sounds like a bestselling game to me, I'm sure Rockstar would snap it up.'

He smiled at her but it didn't reach his eyes. She understood more than he could ever know; she felt it deep inside her. This place was home, not Avaveil itself but the people she was with. Her mother, Connor and even sweet Maggie all held a piece of her heart, but the largest piece belonged to Redka and as she watched his chest rise and fall gently in his deep slumber she worried that she wouldn't be able to break away when she needed to.

***

THE PATH into the woodland village was clear as Connor and Alia approached. The small houses that nestled between the trees were quiet, looking unloved and deserted, not what Connor had been expecting.

'This is odd.' Alia shook her head. 'This village is a thriving centre, it lies midway between the castle and the market town of Delis, it should be busy with fae going about their work.'

Connor drew his sword as they reached the centre of the village; a tall pine tree dominated the clearing, its trunk as wide as a house. A wooden staircase snaked around the trunk of the tree leading to a high tree house hidden amongst the needles.

Alia began to walk up the stairs, her long skirts brushing each step as she went. Connor trailed behind her with his sword still gripped tightly in his hand. They had barely made it up a handful of steps when a voice stopped them.

'Who goes there?'

The voice called down to them from high above. Connor saw a glint of silver and moved to position himself as a shield for the queen.

'Your Queen Alia,' he called out. 'Show yourselves.'

There was movement all around as the fae emerged from their homes and swung from the trees to surround the staircase.

'You lie, our queen is lost to us.'

'She was lost but I rescued her from the demon realm, Phelan.'

There were hushed murmurs all around followed by the sounds of many feet descending the staircase. Connor readied himself for a fight but Alia laid a hand on his shoulder.

'Do not fear, Connor, they will know it is me.'

She was right. As soon as the fae lord came into sight he wheezed loudly and dropped to his knees, bowing his head.

'My dear lord, please do not bow to me, we merely seek your assistance.'

They walked down the stairs until they reached the dirt floor of the village's centre. The fae were wary to approach and Connor caught the fear in their eyes as they stood in small groups.

***

THE FAE lord was a stout man with a ruddy complexion. He rushed to Alia's side and grasped her hands between his own.

'It's a miracle, a sign from the woodland spirits. They have returned you to us in our darkest hour.'

The queen surveyed the village: the fae huddled together in family groups, mothers clinging to their children, husbands clinging to their wives, the older members of the community sheltering behind the young. There was no evidence of the vitality, the power and the glow of the fae in these people.

'What has happened here?'

The lord bowed his head once more, and feelings of sadness and grief washed over his aura in waves. Connor could feel the man's energies, could sense the desolation in his heart.

'My dear queen, Avaveil is a very different place since you last ruled on the throne. I think it may be best to get under cover before we tell you what has become of your realm.'

He began to walk up the spiral staircase and motioned for Alia and Connor to join him. They walked in silence as the fae from the village vanished quickly into their hiding places.

Connor felt a sense of dread coat his skin as he ascended the stairs to the lord's tree house.

THE SPICED tea warmed them as they sat around the open fire in the circular room. The lord had sent his guards to the outskirts of the village to post a lookout.

'Why do you need to guard the village?' Connor asked as he sipped at his tea.

'If Princess Nikita suspects that you are here, she will burn my village to the ground and leave no survivors.'

'Who is Nikita?'

Alia got up and walked to stand in front of the fire. She stared into the flames as she answered Connor's question. 'Nikita is my sister.'

'Why would she burn the village? Surely she'll be pleased to see that you are safe and back to take over the realm?'

The lord shook his head. 'Princess Nikita is not like our queen, she doesn't have a compassionate bone in her body. The realm was overjoyed when we learned that our queen was with child, we hoped for a future king, one who would ensure that Nikita never made it to the throne. But on that fateful night our beloved queen was taken from the castle. The guards searched the lands for months, and the people never gave up hope, but Princess Nikita stepped up to rule in Queen Alia's stead and ravaged the lands.'

Connor watched as Alia's shoulders shook. She braced her hands against the hearth of the fire and let out a wracking sob.

'My queen, I am so sorry to be the one to break this news to you.' The lord bowed his head again and offered her more tea.

'If Alia is the rightful queen, then all we have to do is walk into the castle and tell her sister that her time is up.'

'Getting into the castle is no longer possible,' he said, shaking his head. 'Princess Nikita has destroyed the surrounding towns and villages, the castle stands like a beacon of terror in the middle of our realm. She trades with orcs and necromancers, selling our resources to fund her materialistic whims. She sells our people as slaves to the Minotaurs from the desert plains and consorts with dark magic practitioners.'

Connor looked across at Alia, his jaw rigid as he saw the pain carved on her face.

'We have just escaped one evil realm, and it appears that I have brought you into another.' Her tears tumbled down her face as she gazed into Connor's eyes.

'The throne of Avaveil is yours by right and when you have no passion left to rule you can hand over to Redka, that's your heritage. I'm half fae so your path is linked to mine. Myanna, Amber and even Tom have followed you here because we believe in you.'

The lord looked at Connor with a quizzical expression 'Who are these people you talk of?'

Connor addressed the lord. 'Myanna is a witch who nursed your queen in Phelan and saved her life, Amber and Tom are from the human realm and...well, that's another story, but Redka, well he is Alia's son, born in Phelan but heir to Avaveil's throne and as I'm here with time on my hands, then I for one intend to help your queen and her band of merry men reclaim her throne.'

The squat little lord clapped his hands and beamed at Connor. 'I haven't heard such passion and fire for so long. Nikita told us that both our queen and her child were lost to us.' He bowed to Alia. 'My queen, do you really think that your band of warriors can help us return Avaveil to its former glory?'

'My son is wounded, my lord, and we are all weak. If you can offer us shelter and assistance then, yes, I believe it may be time to reclaim my throne.'

'We would be honoured to assist you, my queen. You will reside here in my tree house, and the villagers will fetch you everything you need.'

'So be it. We will need men to carry my son's stretcher and food, bedding and herbs. We are camped in a small clearing just south of your village in the west woods.'

The lord bounded to his feet. 'Then we must hurry, my queen. Nikita has spies everywhere and I fear that the longer your warriors are out in the open the easier it will be for her to find them.'

THE RUSTLING of branches and cracking of twigs stirred Amber into action. She concealed Redka's body with fallen leaves until he looked nothing more than a part of the undergrowth and then signalled for the others to hide behind the trees surrounding the clearing.

Myanna had stamped out the fire, digging up the earth to bury the embers before covering the whole area with moss and sticks and hiding with the others behind the trees.

The figure that broke into the clearing startled Amber. She pressed her hands to her mouth to stop herself from crying out and squatted lower to the ground. He didn't look like a faerie. Apart from Connor having brown hair due to his part-witch heritage, Amber understood that all fae had white hair. This figure had a shock of bright red hair which hung in lank tendrils around an unshaved face, and a deep scar running down the side of his face from above his eyebrow to his chin. He was carrying a heavy axe in one hand and a dirty sack in the other.

He sniffed the air and turned full circle, moving towards Redka's camouflaged body. Amber braced herself, ready to spring forward. She slid a small dagger that Connor had given her from her belt and prepared herself to strike.

As the red-haired man hovered just above the pile of leaves, an arrow whistled through the trees and embedded itself deep in the man's chest. He flew backwards from the force, dead before his body hit the ground.

Amber sank to her knees as she saw Connor and Alia burst into the clearing followed by twenty fae men with bows and arrows. Myanna rushed forward and embraced Alia then brushed the leaves from Redka's body to show her he was safe.

A stout man with red cheeks gripped Myanna's hands in greeting as Amber walked into the clearing with Tom and Maggie close behind.

Connor appeared at her side, an odd expression on his face.

'What is it?' she asked, almost too afraid to hear the answer.

She looked over his shoulder at Alia who was talking to her mother in a very animated fashion. Four of the fae had lifted Redka from the ground and were hurrying out of the clearing behind the stout man as Alia ushered the others to follow.

'We have to leave *now*,' he said, gesturing for her to go after the retreating group.

'What's going on, Connor?'

He looked at her for a long moment, gazing into her dark brown eyes with such intensity. 'Let's just say we won't be going back home anytime soon.'

The End

About the Author

Shelley Wilson's love of fantasy began at the tender age of eight when she followed Enid Blyton up a Magical Faraway Tree.

Inspired by Blyton's make believe world, Shelley began to create her stories, weaving tales around faeries, witches and dragons.

Writing has always been Shelley's first love, but she has also enjoyed a variety of job roles along the way; from waitressing to sales and marketing and even working as a turkey plucker.

Shelley lives in the West Midlands, UK with her three teenage children, two fish and a dragon called Roger. She is at her happiest with a slice of pizza in one hand, a latte in the other and *Game of Thrones* on the TV. She would love to live in the Shire but fears her five foot ten inch height may cause problems. She is an obsessive list writer, huge social media addict and a full-time day dreamer.